BLOOD PEARL

Camillography Volume 1

Anne Billson

By the same author:

Novels
Dream Demon (a novelisation)
Suckers
Stiff Lips
The Ex
The Coming Thing
The Half Man

Non-Fiction
Screen Lovers
My Name is Michael Caine
The Thing (BFI Modern Classics)
Buffy the Vampire Slayer (BFI TV Classics)
Let The Right One In (Devil's Advocates)
Billson Film Database
Cats on Film

e-books
Breast Man: A Conversation with Russ Meyer

ISBN-10: 1725737094
ISBN-13: 978-1725737099

BLOOD PEARL

Chapter 1
Worse than a Death Warrant

No one had warned Millie Greenwood that vampires and zombies and shapeshifters weren't just mythological creatures, but existed alongside her in the real world. How was she supposed to know that all it would take for them to be after her blood was one stupid signature?

Later on, when she was running for her life, Millie made a valiant effort to look on the bright side. At least that life was no longer boring. But sometimes she couldn't help yearning for everything to be back the way it had been before. It might have been dull, but it had also been safe, and Paula had still been alive.

Forging the signature was the first wilfully disobedient thing Millie had ever done, but in the nearly sixteen years she had been on earth she had been well protected, perhaps excessively so, and no one had told her the truth about the village, or her parents, or the seal. So she had no way of knowing that signing that form was as good as signing her own death warrant.

If you could even call it death, that is, because the fate the Syndicate had in mind for her was far worse.

Until the day when everything changed, Millie's entire experience of the outside world was limited to what she'd read in books or seen on the internet. She spent most of her free time stuck in her bedroom, and there wasn't much to do there except read or browse, unless she felt like gazing out of the window, which made her feel like the Lady of Shalott in the poem by Alfred Lord Tennyson, watching the world go by but forbidden to take part in it.

Except that Millie wasn't cursed, at least not in the way that she thought, and, unlike the Lady of Shalott, she didn't have to look into the mirror to see the view. She could lean out with her elbows on the windowsill and take deep breaths of fresh air. Weather permitting, anyway; for obvious reasons she preferred not to lean out during thunderstorms or blizzards. Not that Bramblewood had a lot of those. Extreme weather conditions would have been just too exciting for the world's most boring village.

As for the world going by, there was never much of that either. The only action, if you could call it that, was the aimless paddling of the ducks in the pond on the village green. And if the term 'village green' makes you think of picture postcards or period films set in country houses, with the local gentry playing cricket and having la-di-da picnics, waited on by servants, or dancing around maypoles, think again. Bramblewood village green was a triangle of scrubby yellow grass with a large dent in the middle that filled up with water whenever it rained. The pond itself was muddy, and the ducks were dodgy-looking.

Millie wasn't even sure they *were* ducks - they were dull brown and scrawny, with curved beaks like tiny scimitars, and jerky head movements, and beady eyes that seemed always to be fixed on her, no matter where she was standing in relation to them. She had once tried searching for the species on a wildlife website, but the only picture she found that was even remotely similar wasn't of a bird at all, but a rare species of Indonesian lizard that had long ago become extinct. Those ducks weren't mallards, that was for sure. She never saw them flying, but whenever anyone went anywhere near their precious pond they flapped their wings and made whistling noises so shrill she had to block her ears.

It wasn't as though there were a lot of people going near the pond, though. Even the Lady of Shalott got to see knights in shining armour, and troops of damsels, and curly shepherd lads passing by, and there would undoubtedly have been all manner of colourful medieval goings-on in the background: maybe Shalott village fêtes with fortune-tellers and coconut shies, and guess the weight of the hey nonny cake competitions.

But there were never any fêtes in Bramblewood, and the only passers-by Millie ever saw were Mr. Figgs the postman, who was so old it took him most of the day to hobble all the way around The Noose (as the road around the green was called) to deliver a handful of letters to the cluster of houses and small businesses. Or Mrs. Crumley, flipping the sign on her shop door from 'CLOSED' to 'OPEN' and then, at five o'clock, back to 'CLOSED' again, except for Saturdays, when she would turn the sign to 'CLOSED' at lunchtime. Or Dr. Scott, who looked in need of medical assistance himself, shuffling past Millie's house on his way to treat a neighbour's gout, or rheumatism, or lumbago, or some other geriatric complaint.

And that was about as thrilling as it got. And yes, Millie did sometimes wonder why she was the only person in the village under retirement age. Even Esther Haze's son, Patrick, had to be at least sixty years old, and Millie dreaded to think how old Mrs. Haze was. Over a hundred, probably. There had surely been younger people living in Bramblewood at some point, but Millie could only assume they'd decided to move somewhere more exciting, like Croydon.

*****

Forging the signature might have been the worst thing she had ever done, but it wasn't as though it was going to harm anyone, or even inconvenience them. She was good little Millie Greenwood, kept herself to herself and worked hard - but not *too* hard - and it helped that she had Paula in her corner. Millie had always had a knack for fading into the wallpaper, and most of her classmates, she suspected, didn't really notice she was there. Apart from Nate McIntyre, of course; he *always* noticed her. But she tried not to think about him.

So no, she didn't get out much. But the day trip to Paris was a chance she couldn't pass up. She'd read *The Hunchback of Notre-Dame* and *The Phantom of the Opera* and *The Three Musketeers*, and a few other books set in Paris by dead French writers whom everyone except Aunt Tanith had told her she wouldn't understand. In fact she'd understood them perfectly well, though of course she'd read the English translations, not the original French. She was good at French, but not *that* good.

But Millie knew there was no point in asking her parents to sign the permission slip. They would say no, just as they always did when she asked them if she could go somewhere on her own. She hardly bothered to ask any more, because she always knew what the answer would be.

Even when she went to the big bookshop in town to stock up on reading material, one of her parents would always come along and hover like a prison guard as she picked up books and read the blurbs, as if they thought they had only to turn their backs for a nanosecond and she would immediately drop the book and run away to London and become a drug addict. (In fact, she did sometimes fantasise about running away to London, though she had no intention of becoming a drug addict. In her fantasies she would end up as a famous actress, or a famous writer, or a famous artist.)

Bramblewood was so boring that Millie actually looked forward to going to school every day. Mallory Hall was just about the only place she didn't have her parents breathing down her neck all the time, though she sensed they would have tagged along and done precisely that, if only school regulations had permitted it.

Every weekday morning, one of her parents would escort her to the pick-up point where she would catch the bus, and then one of them would be waiting for her there when the bus returned to drop her off at the end of the afternoon, which meant she could never slip away to the Five-Star café, where nearly everyone else from her class went after school. The only way she could have gone there was with her parents in tow, which would have made her a laughing stock. Nate McIntyre already called her 'Princess Precious' or 'Mummy's Girl' or 'Stuck-Up Bitch'. Paula was always telling Millie to ignore him, but the nicknames still stung, especially when they made other people snigger.

Thank heavens for Paula, who made sure no one ever pushed Millie around, even though she was always among the last to be chosen when the captains were picking teams at games, and most people dismissed her as a nerd. Millie didn't think she was a hardcore nerd though, not like Julia Evans or Andrew Quigley, who wrote notes to each other in runes they'd taught themselves from the books of J. R. R. Tolkien. Millie had enjoyed *The Hobbit* and *Lord of the Rings*, but not so much that they made her want to learn elvish. She already had enough on her plate with French.

She did sometimes wonder how she'd ended up with someone as amazing as Paula for a friend. Their two personalities couldn't have been more different. Paula was blonde and an extrovert and liked to flirt, and she was really, really popular. If she'd been a character in a Hollywood teen movie, she would have been Head Cheerleader, or Prom Queen. She somehow managed to be an honorary member of all the coolest social cliques without having to pledge herself to any one of them exclusively.

Everyone wanted to be Paula's friend, so Millie could never quite believe her luck that Paula chose to hang out with *her*, of all people. Paula said this was because Millie was smart and funny and made her laugh, even if it wasn't always on purpose. Paula assured Millie she had 'hidden depths' and that one day everyone else would see them too. Which was a pretty cool thing to be told, Millie thought, though she wasted more time than was necessary wondering what you would call 'hidden depths' once they were out in the open.

The highlight of Millie's week was going round to Paula's house, which she did most Saturdays, but even then her mother and father (it didn't seem right to call them 'mum' and 'dad') insisted on driving right up to Paula's house to drop her off. Then they picked her up again before nightfall, because heaven forbid she should be allowed out on her own after dark.

On one occasion, she and Paula made plans to go swimming, but Mrs. O'Keefe, Paula's mother, told them it was out of the question. So swimming was cancelled, and the two girls had stayed in and watched television instead.

'I'm so sorry, Millie,' said Mrs. O'Keefe. 'I know it's unfair, but if I let you go your parents will never allow you to come here again.' There had been a faraway look in her eyes as she'd said this, as though she were trying and failing to dredge up a memory from the distant past. She'd been so apologetic that Millie hadn't liked to make a fuss, but she'd felt like screaming in frustration all the same.

Why couldn't her parents be more like Paula's? Mrs. O'Keefe let Paula go wherever she wanted, within reason, and was always hugging her. Sometimes she hugged Millie too, which just made Millie wonder why her own mother never did that.

But it wasn't just the hugging, or lack of it. Looking back on it later, Millie couldn't remember ever having seen either of her parents smile. They didn't talk to her that much either, though she supposed it could have been worse; at least they weren't violent or abusive, like the Parents from Hell she sometimes read about, and they were the opposite of neglectful, so it seemed churlish to complain.

And though they insisted she went with them to church every Sunday morning, they weren't religious fanatics, like the mother in *Carrie*. (Stephen King was one of Millie's favourite writers, by the way; it wasn't as though she read nothing but high-tone literary classics.)

Millie didn't particularly *enjoy* going to church, a big old draughty place with a steeple like a witch's hat, and much too large for the number of villagers, who rattled around in it like ball bearings in an empty biscuit tin. But she didn't try to get out of it. It seemed important to her parents that she accompany them, and the villagers were always delighted to see her, and sometimes even presented her with small gifts. She tried to be grateful, though to be honest, they were never things she wanted or needed. Drusilla Metford, from the pub, gave her a pack of playing cards, Quentin Withers a set of dessert forks, and Gwen and Freddy Curd solemnly handed her an old wooden animal that was meant to be either a goat or a cat, it wasn't clear which, though it was obviously meant for someone much younger than Millie, who thanked them politely and promptly tucked it away at the back of her wardrobe, out of sight.

Mr. Greenwood worked for an insurance company in Sevenoaks, though he spent more time typing reports or making telephone calls in his study at home than at the office. He never talked about work, and Millie never asked about it, partly because she was sure the answer would be boring. In his spare time, he liked pulling up weeds in the garden, or nailing bits of wood together in the shed, and she always thought it odd that he never changed out of his navy blue suit into something more casual, not even to dig up flowerbeds. She couldn't remember ever having seen him wearing anything other than a suit. Once she'd peeked into her parents' wardrobe and found half a dozen identical navy blue suits hanging in a row. They weren't even stylish - just the kind of suits you might see for sale in inexpensive chain store windows.

As for Mrs. Greenwood, she was nearly always dressed in a grey pleated skirt and white blouse with a pussycat bow. Sometimes she wore an apron to cook or bake, or do housework. Both Millie's parents watched a lot of television, with what seemed to Millie to be an unusual degree of concentration. They stared wide-eyed at the screen, as if trying to absorb and memorise every detail of the local news or weather forecasts.

They fed her reasonably well, albeit not very excitingly, and looked after her just fine. Her mother took her shopping for clothes in one of the nearby towns, only occasionally vetoing a garment on the grounds that it would attract the wrong sort of attention. But Millie was OK with that, because she was a bit shy and didn't feel comfortable standing out from the crowd. (And yes, she was aware she would have to work on that shyness if she was going to be a famous actress.)

Millie's ten pounds a week pocket money wouldn't have lasted two minutes if she'd been leading a normal life, like Paula, who had to supplement her own generous allowance with holiday jobs. But the only place Millie was allowed out on her own was Boringwood, and the only things to visit there were Brenda's Beauty Salon (which was out of the question since Millie had no intention of getting a little old lady perm like the rest of the clientèle) and the pub, which was called, with startling originality, The Bramblewood Arms.

Millie had never been in the pub and neither, as far as she knew, had her parents, who never touched alcohol. And The Bramblewood Arms always seemed to be packed with geriatric villagers drinking and smoking and singing along to old pop songs, so it wasn't exactly on the list of places she was dying to visit. The villagers continued to smoke in the pub long after smoking in public places had been officially outlawed, so that was another strike against it. From her bedroom window, Millie could sometimes see clouds of greyish-yellow smoke escaping through the doorway whenever anyone went in or out.

In short, the only place in the village where one might spend pocket money was Mrs. Crumley's shop, which was full of tinned soup and packets of the dullest type of biscuit. The most interesting thing about the shop was an oddly shaped bulge in the wall, as though a giant fist had tried to punch a hole through it. Mrs. Crumley had been obliged to arrange her shelving on either side of it. Millie had asked her once about the bulge; Mrs. Crumley had muttered something about teenagers, but since the only teenager for miles was Millie herself, who had never punched anything even if she'd sometimes felt like it, she didn't find the answer very illuminating.

The only items in the shop worth buying were magazines and chocolate (and Millie sometimes rented DVDs, though the selection was limited to family films and romantic comedies) so she had managed to save most of her pocket money. She kept the notes rolled up in a green glass jar decorated with gold and scarlet swirls, and kept the jar hidden behind some books, though wasn't sure why she bothered, as she'd never heard of any the houses in Bramblewood getting burgled.

So by the time the notice about the day trip to Paris went up on the notice board at school, she already knew she had enough money to pay for it. The only problem was the consent form, which was supposed to be signed by one of her parents so that her name could be included on the travel documents for the handful of pupils who hadn't already got their own passports.

'Tell them it's educational,' said Paula. 'You'll be able to practise your French. You never know, they *might* say yes.'

Millie sighed. 'They won't let me go to the swimming pool on my own. You think they'll let me go abroad? Even for just one day?'

'But you won't be on your own. There'll be teachers, unfortunately. And you'll be with me. And Philip and Sam. Let me repeat that. Sam! Oh yes, you know he likes you.'

She nudged Millie with her elbow, though being nudged by Paula always felt like being struck in the ribs by a guided missile. Millie risked a sideways peek at Sam Tulliver, who was on the other side of the classroom, discussing football with Philip Freeman and Coral Baines and, ugh, Nate McIntyre. Millie knew it had to be football they were discussing, because they were all doing that strange ostrich-like thing with their necks which she guessed was boy-mime for heading an invisible ball into an invisible net.

Sam was tall and had fair hair that flopped over his forehead, and an easy smile that made Millie go weak at the knees. He led a charmed life, always getting the winning goal or ending up in the finals of sporting events, which added to his allure, even to people like Millie who had no interest in sport.

She covertly kept an eye on him in class, and loved his rather odd habit of staring intently at inanimate objects such as pencils, or erasers, or pieces of paper, as if trying to divine their secret essence. Since she never went to the Five-Star after school, she'd never really had the chance to talk to him properly, but any time he said anything to her, even just 'Hi!' or 'What room are we in next?', she could feel her face glowing beetroot red. She wished she liked football as much as Coral, because then she and Sam would have had something to talk about.

The fact Sam ever talked to her at all was surprising, because she certainly never said anything clever back, though she always managed to think of a brilliantly witty retort five minutes after he'd moved on. The French had a term for that: *l'esprit de l'escalier* - 'The Spirit of the Staircase'. She wondered what Sam saw in her, if indeed he saw anything at all. She wasn't attractive and outgoing like Paula, or drop-dead sexy like Ayesha Washington, or arty and original, like Alison Moseby. Millie's hair was long but limp, and a browny-black that seemed to soak up the light, rather than reflect it like the hair in shampoo commercials. Her skin was pale, not through choice but because sunbathing made her come out in a rash, and though her eyes were green, it was a drab greyish green, like dishwater, rather than the dazzling emerald she imagined green eyes ought to be.

But she wasn't awful-looking, she thought - so long as she remembered not to scowl, which Paula said was off-putting and even a bit scary, because it made her eyes disappear into pools of shadow.

Millie liked Sam's friend Philip almost as much as she liked Sam, but Philip was off limits, because Paula had been out with him several times and, as she was always saying, you never trespassed on your best friend's territory.

Nate McIntyre, on the other hand, was something else entirely. Millie couldn't understand why Sam and Philip gave him the time of day. Nate wasn't good-natured and easy-going, like them. Nor was he good-looking: he was dark and wiry and intense, not much taller than Millie, and scowled a lot. She sometimes wondered if she looked as ugly and intimidating as Nate when she scowled.

And when Nate wasn't scowling, he had a vicious grin and an even more vicious sense of humour which was often directed at Millie. She couldn't work out why he hated her - she'd never done anything to offend him. But this didn't stop him calling her catty names or making sarcastic comments. Whenever she answered a question in class, he would pull faces and mimic her accent, which he said was posh, though Paula assured Millie it was nothing of the sort.

'Don't worry about it,' Paula said. 'He's just jealous.'

'Why would he be jealous?' Millie asked. 'He doesn't spend his life stuck at home, like me. He can go wherever he likes.'

'Only because his mother couldn't care less what he gets up to,' said Paula. It was true. Everyone knew Nate came from a troubled background; his father had run off years ago, and his uncle was in jail, though no one knew why. Someone said it was for drug dealing, someone else said kidnapping, and there was even a rumour he'd killed someone in a fight. Nate himself had once been picked up by the police for spray-painting graffiti on the school gates, and it was only through the personal intervention of Miss Cooper, the headmistress, that he hadn't been expelled.

'Only a matter of time before he gets himself into serious trouble,' said Paula. 'The worst sort of yob, not worth getting upset about. Ignore him.'

Millie tried to follow Paula's advice, but it wasn't easy when Nate always seemed to be trying to turn people against her. What on earth was his problem?

Paula's theory was that he had a secret crush on Millie, but then Paula had a great many theories relating to love, romance and secret crushes. Millie found most of them naïve and a bit silly, though would never have dreamt of saying so to Paula's face, and had to admit Paula had more experience than she did in affairs of the heart. Paula's favourite reading matter was romantic fiction, often involving doctors and nurses, or heiresses and highwaymen, or schoolgirls who fell passionately in love with pale and interesting vampires who looked like handsome young men but who in reality were hundreds of years old. She'd once lent one of these supernatural romances to Millie, who'd been more disturbed by it than she cared to admit.

'It's creepy,' she said, returning the book to Paula at lunchtime. "This guy is over two hundred years old, and here he is getting mushy with a girl who's only a few years older than we are. He's, like, nearly two hundred years older than she is! Don't you think that's a bit creepy? Why can't he find a girlfriend his own age?'

'But he *looks* young,' said Paula, who had enjoyed the novel very much, and was slightly peeved Millie didn't share her enthusiasm for it. 'And anyway they love each other, so age doesn't matter. Love conquers all.'

'No, it doesn't,' said Millie. 'And anyway that's not the point. He's *old*, don't you see? If he looked anything like his real age, everyone would find their relationship pervy. At least you know where you are with the vampire in *Salem's Lot.* He just wants to bite people. He couldn't care less about having a girlfriend. Not like your guy, pretending to be a teenager when he's not. He's like a paedophile.'

'You just don't get it, do you?' said Paula, exasperated. 'Vampires stop getting older as soon as they're turned into vampires. They're young and beautiful for ever! Imagine! Wouldn't that be great?'

'Maybe not,' said Millie. 'Not if you were stuck with a face you didn't like, and it never changed.'

'But no one wants to grow old.'

'I do,' said Millie. 'I want to be old enough to do what I want.'

'You could do whatever you wanted if you were a vampire,' said Paula.

'That's not true,' said Millie. 'If I were a vampire, I couldn't go out in the daylight. Or cross running water, or eat garlic.' She paused, trying not to frown. 'But this is a completely stupid argument anyway, because there's *no such thing* as vampires.'

They both burst out laughing, and found they couldn't stop. Each time they were on the point of pulling themselves together, Paula would catch Millie's eye, or vice versa, and they would start giggling again, until eventually they'd forgotten why they'd started laughing in the first place.

Inevitably, their laughter attracted the attention of Nate, who sneered at them from the next table. 'You girlies are so cute together. Anyone would think you were lesbians.'

Paula stuck her tongue out and said, 'You wish.'

But Millie stopped laughing, not because of the lesbian remark, but because she was reminded of how Nate always seemed to be spying on her. Maybe Paula was right and he did have a secret crush, though if that was the case he had a funny way of showing it.

In the next break, Millie asked Paula, as casually as she could, 'Nate's not going on the Paris trip, is he?'

'Shouldn't think so,' said Paula. 'His mum's on benefits, so he won't have the money. Unless of course he steals it, which I wouldn't put past him.'

'Because it would really spoil things if he came,' said Millie.

Paula looked at her and let out a little squeal of delight. 'Then you're coming? You really *are* coming?'

'I'm nearly sixteen,' said Millie. 'Boringwood is driving me nuts. They can't keep me cooped up there for ever. I'm fed up with only being able to *read* about the world, Paula. It's time I saw it for myself.'

'What about the permission slip? Did you get them to sign it?'

Millie sighed and shook her head. 'That's the problem. There's no way they'll do that.'

Paula smiled and lent towards her and whispered in her ear, so close that it tickled. 'Maybe *they* won't sign it, my dear, but what about... someone else? What if someone else just happened to have the same handwriting as your mum or dad? It's not as though anyone here would ever spot the difference...'

So it was basically Paula's idea, but she couldn't have predicted the consequences any more than Millie, so there was no point in blaming her when it all went horribly wrong.

Especially considering what happened to her later on.

Chapter 2
The Bats

Finding a sample of her parents' handwriting was easier said than done. Her father did all his writing on a computer, and her mother didn't even do that. Millie had never been away from home for more than a day, so they'd never had occasion to send her letters. Her birthday cards had always just been signed 'Your parents', which obviously wouldn't work; the school would be expecting something a little more specific.

But as is so often the way, Millie found what she was looking for only after she had given up searching for it.

On the day in question, she was round at Aunt Tanith's. Tanith had more than once told Millie to call her just 'Tanith', but Millie felt uncomfortable addressing her aunt by her first name. It seemed disrespectful, somehow.

Tanith was the Greenwoods' next-door neighbour - their houses shared one wall and a chimney breast - and Millie liked to pop round as often as she could. Partly this was because she thought of Tanith as a friend (even though, like all the other villagers, she was several aeons older than Millie) and partly because Millie's parents didn't mind her visiting Tanith any time she liked, nor did they feel the need to escort her there and back.

Besides, Millie felt at home next door. Tanith's house, unlike that of the Greenwoods, was a mess, but an interesting mess, with books and piles of papers and pictures and exotic ornaments strewn all over the place. There was always something to examine or fiddle with. The only thing Millie didn't care for was Tanith's collection of antique dolls, which had blank faces and staring eyes that seemed to follow her around the room.

These were not the kind of dolls Millie had once played with. They were old and fragile, and dressed in rotting lace. Some had limbs missing, or gaping holes where their mouths should have been. One or two, when you turned them upside-down or pressed a button in their stomachs, would say things like 'ma-ma' or 'let me kiss you', which was unbelievably creepy, especially as the speaking devices had warped with age, and the words that came out didn't always sound the way they were supposed to.

Luckily, Tanith kept most of the doll collection in a guest room upstairs, so Millie didn't see it often. Tanith had probably guessed that it creeped her out.

It had been Tanith who had always encouraged Millie to read. Virtually the only books in the Greenwoods' house were the ones in Millie's own bedroom; her parents didn't read much. But nearly every available wall in Tanith's house was crammed with bookshelves, and she enjoyed recommending titles. She also liked to talk about all the travelling she'd done around Europe and Africa and Asia. Millie tried to work out when this had taken place. Judging by the stories, it must have been many years ago, probably long before Millie was born.

But though Millie loved hearing about Tanith's adventures, she couldn't help wondering why anyone who'd been leading such an exciting life would give it up to settle down in Boringwood, of all places. Once or twice Millie had asked her about it, but Tanith had just responded with things like, 'Oh, I just got tired of living out of a suitcase,' or 'I felt like putting down roots,' or once, with a laugh to indicate she was only joking, 'The fate of the world depended on it.' Millie never found such explanations truly satisfying, but they were the only ones she ever got.

Millie had been tempted to confide in Tanith about the Paris trip. Tanith, more than anyone, would surely understand why Millie might want to see the world, even if it required a little dishonesty to do so.

But something held her back. What if her aunt felt it was her duty to tell the Greenwoods? Or worse, what if she *didn't* tell them, and then her parents found out anyway, which would get Tanith into trouble? In the end, Millie decided it was more prudent to stay silent.

But on the afternoon in question, only two days before the deadline for handing in the forms, they were drinking afternoon tea (her aunt always favoured peculiar-tasting blends like Earl Grey or Lapsang Souchong) when Tanith suddenly got it into her head they needed chocolate biscuits as well. So she slipped on her coat and popped out to buy a packet from Mrs. Crumley's.

Millie knew Tanith was pathologically incapable of buying anything from Mrs. Crumley's shop without stopping to chat for at least fifteen minutes, but she didn't mind. She always enjoyed being left on her own in

Tanith's cottage, because it gave her a chance to poke around.

Not that she poked around in her aunt's private possessions, and she would never have dreamt of opening cupboards or drawers, but when Millie was on her own she did everything she felt too self-conscious to do when Tanith was present, such as gazing into the dark engravings of sphinxes and big old buildings that looked like churches but which she somehow knew were not. Or she could flick through some of the antique books filled not only with incomprehensible languages and mathematical formulae, but with fascinating illustrations of mythological animals, or beautiful women in medieval gowns, or old maps of places Millie had never heard of, which were decorated with sea monsters or volcanoes or puffy-cheeked cherubs. Or she could fiddle with the elaborate wooden puzzles, or the pewter animals, or the snow globe Tanith used as a paperweight on her writing desk.

The fact that the globe contained a small-scale replica of the Eiffel Tower might not have been entirely coincidental, Millie realised later.

But that afternoon, as she performed her usual ritual of shaking the globe to make the white flakes swirl lazily around the miniature iron tower, her gaze fell on the pile of papers the paperweight had been pinning down.

The topmost sheet was a short handwritten note.

Millie had no intention of being nosy, but before she could stop herself, she found herself reading it.

'Nothing to report. No sightings. No anomalies. No alarms tripped. All seals intact. Rabbit continues to be amenable.'

The note was signed 'Aurelia Greenwood'.

This was very odd. Millie had no idea what her mother was writing about. Sightings of what? What kind of alarms? There weren't any burglar alarms in Bramblewood, as far as she knew, and there was no need for them anyway since it was almost certainly the village with the lowest crime rate in the world.

And what did her mother mean by 'seals'? Clearly not the semi-aquatic mammals you threw fish to. Perhaps she was referring to those blobs of wax used to secure letters in the days before adhesive envelopes. As for rabbits, Millie had sometimes glimpsed them lolloping through the fields surrounding the village, but why should her mother be concerned about them? Unless, of course, they'd started eating her father's lettuce.

And what did she mean by 'amenable'? Millie knew the word meant something similar to 'amicable' or 'friendly', but without a clear context she couldn't put her finger on the precise sense. She made a mental note to consult her dictionary when she got home.

But of course she forgot. Because the contents of the note weren't nearly as interesting as the way it was written. Up until then she'd been wavering, almost hoping that, despite her earlier bravado, she would have to tell Paula she couldn't go.

But her mother's handwriting was so plain, so almost like printing, that the very sight of it made Millie's mind up for her. It *had* to be a sign. Millie was meant to go to Paris. She was destined to go to Paris. She *would* go to Paris, dammit, and nothing was going to stop her.

And so she pulled out the permission slip she'd been keeping folded like a talisman in her pocket, picked up a pen from Tanith's desk, and, heart in mouth, carefully copied her mother's signature on to the dotted line.

When she'd finished, she set down the pen and, with a certain amount of satisfaction, examined the signature from all angles. It was perfect. It could almost be the real thing!

As she slipped the form back into her pocket, a shiver of excitement went through her. There! She'd done it! She had just crossed a line.

Nothing happened, of course.

At least, not then.

*****

The night before the Paris trip, it was all she could do to act naturally in front of her parents, when what she really wanted was to jump up and down like a six-year-old on a trampoline, shouting, 'I'm going to Paris tomorrow! I'm going to Paris tomorrow!'

She'd already warned them she had to work on a class astronomy project, and so would be required to arrive at Mallory Hall before dawn, which meant the bus would be picking her up earlier than usual. A lot earlier. Even to her own ears this cover story sounded bogus, and she expected her parents to ask for more details, especially when she added that she wouldn't need to wear uniform.

But she had underestimated the Greenwoods' lack of curiosity. They dutifully read her end-of-term reports, and said, 'Well done, Millie!' whenever she got high marks in English or French, but they never, ever asked questions. Not *real* questions. Just polite inquiries as to whether she wanted a cup of tea, or if she needed any clothes washed.

That night she went to bed at nine o'clock, after setting her alarm for the outrageous hour of three in the morning, but she was much too excited to sleep properly. The nearest she came to it was a shallow doze in which she dreamt she was looking out of her bedroom window, but instead of the village green, she was seeing an ocean of sloping silvery-grey rooftops and red chimney pots stretching as far as the eye could see. On the horizon were ranged the unmistakeable shapes of the Eiffel Tower, and Notre-Dame, and the Arc de Triomphe, silhouetted against the setting sun. She wasn't in Bramblewood; she was already in the middle of Paris! And couldn't even remember how she'd got there!

But something was wrong. One minute the sky was blue and pink and warm, the next a glowering dark cloud was spreading across it, casting a cold shadow over the city. Millie felt herself shivering in her half-sleep. And there was something even blacker in the sky - a large flock of birds, wheeling in formation, coming closer and closer. Crows! Millie shrank back, trying to close the window, but couldn't find the catch. And still the flock of crows was coming closer. No, not a flock, she thought, a *murder*. That was what you called it: a *murder* of crows.

Except they weren't crows, she saw that now as they swooped and dived towards her. They were bats. Giant, black bats. And they were coming closer...

Millie jerked awake and rolled on her side to look at the clock. She couldn't believe it was still only half past one. It wasn't surprising she'd dreamt about Paris, because her head was bursting with excitement about the trip. She just hoped it wasn't going to be full of bats when she got there.

Don't be silly, she told herself sternly. Of course Paris wouldn't be full of bats. They were just symbols, she decided. Probably anxiety about deceiving her parents bubbling up from her subconscious. Dreams never showed you reality, she knew. Besides, she'd pored over enough maps of the city to be pretty sure the Eiffel Tower and Notre-Dame weren't *that* close to each other.

She decided she didn't want to go back to sleep anyway, not if it meant dreaming about bats. So she lay staring at the gently shifting shadows on the ceiling, cast there by light filtering through her curtains from the single lamppost in the middle of the green. She thought about Paris and wondered if it would live up to her expectations, which she was aware were excessively romantic. Maybe it would turn out to be a grubby little city full of ugly architecture and horrible people and ghastly food.

Maybe. But somehow she didn't think so.

By the time the alarm went off, she was already wide-awake. She had carefully laid out her clothes the night before, taking the trouble to put together an outfit she hoped would make her look cool without giving the impression she'd tried too hard. Her best black jeans, white T-shirt with a picture of an eight-armed Indian goddess on the front, and her most comfortable trainers, because she expected there to be a lot of walking. She also knew it would be chilly at this time of year. From the window she could already see fingers of early morning mist curling around the green, so she chose the warmer of her two jackets - a quilted one in olive green, with a hood in case it rained - and her favourite red scarf, which she had knitted herself, and which was long enough to wind several times around the lower part of her face if it turned out to be really cold.

She stowed what remained of her pocket money in the small tan leather backpack Tanith had given her for her birthday, and which she normally kept for special occasions, not that there were many of those in Bramblewood. She wondered if her parents would want to know why she was taking it to school today, but decided probably not, not if past form was anything to go by. They didn't seem curious about her at all.

She had washed her hair the previous evening, and now it was sticking out all over the place, as though she'd stuck her finger in an electric socket. She combed anti-frizz product through it and dragged it back into a ponytail. There were still a few tendrils escaping, but at least when she examined herself in the mirror she didn't look too much like a mad gorgon. The only bad thing was a spot on her chin, but once she'd covered it with concealer it was almost invisible.

She stared into the mirror, trying to look at herself through Sam's eyes. What did he see when he looked at her? What did any of them see? She wasn't anywhere near as gorgeous or glamorous or fabulous as Paula or Ayesha or Katy, but maybe she didn't look so bad. Just as long as she remembered not to scowl. Millie practised not scowling into the mirror. The results were encouraging.

On regular school mornings, one of her parents would walk her to the bus stop, but when she got downstairs she found both of them fully dressed and waiting, almost as though they'd never gone to bed in the first place.

Her mother said, 'Good morning, Millie,' as she always did, and handed Millie a small plastic bag; 'Sandwiches and orange juice. For later.'

Millie thanked her, touched by her mother's thoughtfulness. It was still so early that the very thought of eating breakfast made her feel slightly sick, but she guessed she would be hungry later on.

She stood on tiptoe to kiss Mrs. Greenwood's cheek. Later, she would regret not having given her a great big hug as well, even though she knew her mother didn't do hugs. But by then it would be too late.

There were few signs of life in the village as the three of them crossed the green on their way to the bus stop, though the ducks made their usual peculiar high-pitched whistling as they walked past the pond, and there was a light in one of the windows of the St. Leonard's annex. As they approached it, Millie heard the deep, echoing bark of Reverend Pardew's Great Dane. Millie usually liked dogs, but this one gave her the willies; it was like the Hound of the Baskervilles.

What could the Reverend be up to at this hour? Probably writing one of his excruciatingly long and tedious sermons, by far the worst part of the Sunday service. Pardew was Millie's least favourite villager. He was tall and gaunt, with unkempt beetle-brows and flapping garments that made him look a scarecrow, and he didn't so much walk as stalk, like someone wearing stilts. It wasn't just his appearance, though; sometimes, in mid-service, Millie would catch him glaring at her as though he were compiling a mental list of all the sins she had ever committed. Which always made her uneasy, even though she had never done anything *really* bad.

Until now, that is. What would the Reverend say if he found out about her forging that signature? It didn't bear thinking about.

But then they were past the annex and down Ferret Lane to the pick-up point. As always, the bus rolled up thirty seconds after they'd reached it. Not for the first time, Millie wondered if her parents were equipped with some kind of bus radar. Their timing was always spot on, even when they left the house late or, on one occasion, five minutes earlier than usual. How on earth had they predicted the bus would be early that morning? It had to be an amazing coincidence. One of a long series of coincidences. Millie's head hurt just thinking about it.

The bus door slid open with a hiss. Millie said goodbye and clambered aboard, a part of her still worrying that her parents would suddenly do something wildly out of character, such as talk to the driver or Mrs. Fletcher, discover the truth, and haul her back to Bramblewood. She smiled nervously at Mrs. Fletcher, who was sitting behind the driver. Mrs. Fletcher blearily nodded back and jotted something down on a clipboard.

Meanwhile, Paula was flapping her arms to attract Millie's attention, which was unnecessary since she was sitting near the door and her pink jacket made her impossible to overlook. Paula was a big fan of pink, but the jacket was made of such thin fabric that Millie was a little surprised to see her friend wearing it on such a chilly morning.

Paula patted the empty seat next to her, and said, 'Thank goodness you're here!' as Millie sat down. 'This lot are no fun at all.'

Millie turned and saw Rosie Driscoll and Alison Moseby fast asleep in the seat behind them. Nearly everyone else appeared to be out for the count as well. One or two of her classmates were snoring gently.

As the bus started off again, Millie looked out of the window at her parents, side by side at the edge of the road. There was something unnatural about the way they were standing - ramrod straight, arms dangling at their sides, and staring up at her with an expression of loss, as though their lives simply weren't worth living when Millie wasn't there, and would continue to be not worth living right up until the moment they laid eyes on her again.

But if they missed her that badly, Millie thought, why did they never tell her so, or say they loved her, or any of the things that other parents said to their children? Still, she knew they wouldn't budge from their roadside position until the bus had disappeared over the hill, which was slightly annoying, but also quite comforting. Millie felt another twinge of guilt about deceiving them, and forced herself to smile and wave goodbye, feeling guiltier still when they both raised their arms, a little stiffly, and waved back.

The bus picked up speed as it passed the sign: YOU ARE NOW LEAVING BRAMBLEWOOD. DRIVE SAFELY.'

And then it had reached the tree-lined stretch of road leading to Cutter's Peak, and turned on to the trunk road leading not just to Mallory Hall, but also to London, and Mr. and Mrs. Greenwood were lost to sight.

Millie felt a flash of panic, as though she'd done something terrible, something she would never be able to undo, but then Paula was talking to her about the TV sitcom they'd both watched the night before, and Millie forgot her misgivings and began to relax.

After a while, Paula stopped talking, and when Millie glanced sideways she saw that Paula too had fallen asleep. Even with her mouth hanging open, she looked pretty.

Millie was too excited to sleep. She gazed out of the window at the dark countryside, which eventually gave way to Greater London, and then to London itself. There wasn't much traffic around at this hour, so progress was smooth.

It was still dark when they arrived at St. Pancras International. It wasn't the first time Millie had been to London, but it was the first time she'd been there without her parents, and the first time she'd seen the station with its Gothic arches and spiky clock tower. The grim outline against the sky made her think of the haunted mansions she'd read about in books, but once she and her classmates had been herded off the bus and into the station itself, she found the interior was modern and brightly lit, not at all like something out of a ghost story.

Most of her fellow travellers were yawning, and some were almost sleepwalking as Mrs. Fletcher and Mr. Ryan (who looked only half-awake themselves) led everyone through to the Eurostar terminal, where they met up with Miss Brown and a handful of pupils who had been dropped off at the station by their parents. Everyone started stocking up on hot drinks and sodas and breakfast pastries from the only snack bar that was open, but Millie decided she didn't need anything else to eat or drink; she already had her sandwiches and juice, and she wanted to keep what was left of her money and change it into euros, for later. She was determined to buy a souvenir. Maybe a snow globe with a miniature Eiffel Tower inside it, like Tanith's.

As she and a somnolent Paula lined up in front of the gates, Millie caught sight of Sam up ahead and her heart skittered excitedly. There were only half a dozen people between them. Maybe she and Sam would end up sitting near each other on the train. The idea made her so nervous she found herself almost wishing she had stayed at home, but the feeling passed in the blink of an eye. This was it then. This was the big adventure!

She felt a hand fasten on to her arm. Paula had snapped out of her trance, somehow managing to pass from semi-comatose to wide-awake without going through any of the intermediate stages of dawning consciousness.

'Well, my dear,' she said brightly. 'Ready to say goodbye to England?'

'You bet,' said Millie. 'Though "see you later" might be more appropriate, since it's only a day trip.'

'Hoping to meet some nice young French hombres?'

'That's Spanish. You mean *hommes*.'

'Don't be so fussy. You know what I mean.'

'Let's not get ahead of ourselves,' said Millie. 'I haven't even met any nice young English men.'

'Oh, I daresay we can remedy that,' Paula said, and winked.

It was then that things began to go horribly wrong.

Millie was still keeping half an eye on Sam, who was talking to someone up ahead. But only now did the people blocking her sightline shift position enough to let her see who Sam was talking to. It wasn't Philip, as she'd assumed. It was Nate McIntyre.

'Oh no,' she whispered, feeling as if someone had poured a bucket of freezing water over her.

Paula followed her gaze, saw the problem, and promptly switched into authoritative mode. 'Now, don't let him spoil things for you. He'll only upset you if you *allow* him to upset you.'

Millie knew Paula was right, but as the first set of pupils began to filter though the gates, Nate turned back, as if to take one last look at the station behind him. He too seemed only half-awake, but the instant he laid eyes on Millie his jaw dropped open and his face turned a ghastly ashen grey.

For a moment he and Millie just stood and stared at each other. She wanted nothing more than to turn her back on him and pretend he wasn't there, but their eyes seemed to be locked together and she was unable to tear her gaze away.

Nate was the first to move. With a visible shudder, he ripped himself free of the spell and started yelling.

'Millie Greenwood! What the *hell* do you think you're doing?'

Chapter 3
The Tunnel

Everyone was staring at Millie, who felt herself blushing to the roots of her hair. She managed to squeeze out the words, 'I've as much right to be here as you have.' But her voice sounded feeble, even to her own ears, and she wasn't sure it had carried far enough for Nate to hear. In any case, he kept shouting.

'Does Miss Cooper know? What about mummy and daddy? Do they know their precious baby bird has flown the coop?'

Millie wanted the ground to split open and swallow her up. And still Nate kept yelling. 'How in hell did you manage to get permission? What were your parents *thinking*?'

Millie caught her breath. Did he know she had forged that signature? Was this public humiliation the universe's way of punishing her? Everyone was looking from Millie to Nate and back again to Millie, eager to see how she would react. She felt her bottom lip tremble, and told herself sternly not to make things even more embarrassing by bursting into tears.

She'd forgotten Paula was on her team. Her best friend had been slow to size up the situation, but now she more than made up for it. 'Millie's parents are OK with it, but thank you for your concern,' Paula said in the clear, ringing tones that had landed her leading roles in the last two school plays.

It wasn't enough to defuse the situation, but Millie felt thankful she wasn't alone. Because now she saw with a sinking feeling that Nate was on the move. He was coming towards them, roughly bundling out of the way anyone who happened to be standing in his path. Kevin Marshall, who didn't like being bundled, swore and punched him on the shoulder as he passed, but Nate ignored him and continued to advance, until he was planted right in front of Millie, so close that it made her want to step backwards, out of range. But she knew she couldn't give an inch, or it would all be over.

'You are *not* coming,' he said. 'You *can't* come. You stupid, stupid girl, do you have any idea what would happen if you got on that train?'

One or two people in earshot giggled, thinking this was another of Nate's habitual be-mean-to-Millie jokes. But Millie could see he was serious, which was even more troubling than his usual sarcasm. In fact he was frowning so intently she could no longer see his eyes, which had disappeared into pools of black shadow. Was that what *she* looked like when she frowned, she wondered. She realised she was actually feeling a little frightened of him.

Paula snorted, though not because she was amused. 'What's it to you, asshole? Why should you care? This is a free country, and as far as I know France is too. Millie can go wherever she likes.'

"That's just it! She *can't!*

The pitch of Nate's voice rose several levels until it sounded as if he were being strangled. His face was turning from grey to angry pink. He started frantically turning his head from side to side, reminding Millie of the birds on the duck pond.

Then, to her dismay, she realised he was looking for a teacher. He was preparing to make a scene even bigger than the one he was making already.

She wanted to run away and hide. This was getting more awful by the second. What if Mrs. Fletcher or Mr. Ryan or Miss Brown started asking difficult questions? What if, horror of horrors, they phoned her parents? The adventure would be over before it had even begun, and they'd never let her out of their sight again, not even for a moment. She would grow old and grey in Bramblewood, a prisoner in her own house.

Millie heard Mr. Ryan's booming but kindly voice somewhere behind her - 'Come along now, no lollygagging' - and decided she had no intention of sticking around long enough to find out what Nate's problem was, or what he wanted or didn't want. He was stretching his arms out in front of her, like a goalkeeper trying to block her shot. Millie had never much cared for sports, but she did like dancing, even if it was only on her own, in her bedroom, when a song she liked came on the radio. So she feinted, as if to go left. But as soon as Nate had committed himself to that direction, she swivelled smartly, and went the other way.

It was a nifty manoeuvre, and she felt a twinge of pride at a job well done. Paula must have enjoyed it too, because she clapped her hands and shouted, 'Olé!'

They could still hear Nate yelling, but now his voice was bouncing uselessly off their backs, and Millie was feeling bullish and refused to look round at him. She took the path he had cleared earlier, which helped her jump nearly to the head of the queue - it was easy because everyone was still standing around gawping at him - and before she knew it she had caught up with Sam and was following him through the gate, with Paula bringing up the rear.

Millie heard Nate yelling, 'Stop her! She's got a bomb!' But then she, Paula and Sam were diving through the sliding doors, Paula and Millie laughing with relief as they slipped out of their jackets and posted them, with their bags, through the security machine.

The opaque glass doors continued to slide open and closed behind them as other pupils trickled through in ones and twos. Millie could still hear Nate shouting, but his voice was no longer the only one raised. She thought she recognised Mr. Ryan's, though she'd never heard him so angry before. She mentally crossed her fingers, hoping he wasn't taking Nate's side. She could also hear barking, but didn't have time to stand around wondering about whose dogs they were, because now she, Paula and Sam were being ushered directly through passport control, where Miss Brown was waiting, diligently counting heads and making marks on her clipboard as they passed.

Millie felt a sense of accomplishment at having passed the first big obstacle, though she was still a little shaken as well. She'd known Nate didn't like her - he'd always made that fairly obvious, after all - but she had never imagined him capable of blowing his top like that.

'What's up with McIntyre?' asked Bonetta Reese.

'Probably trying to smuggle drugs,' Alison Moseby said nastily, which was rich coming from her, Millie thought. Alison and Bonetta were unofficial members of the Nate McIntyre Fan Club, always ready to lead the sniggering when he made unpleasant cracks at Millie's expense.

And then Sam turned and said, right to Millie's face, 'Poor Nate. He really does seem to have a thing about you, doesn't he?'

And he smiled his warm and fabulous smile, and Millie was walking on air all the way up the escalator to the platform where the train was waiting.

*****

Paula's marks at school tended to be average, at best, and most of the teachers thought she was lazy, which Millie supposed might have been true when it came to things like homework and exams. But Millie also supposed it didn't matter too much, because Paula made up for it in other ways. For example, she had an enviable talent for arranging things to her best advantage, which Millie reckoned would eventually stand her in better stead than any number of certificates or academic qualifications.

Sure enough, with her customary self-assurance, Paula smoothly commandeered a set of face-to-face seating in the middle of the carriage, and made sure she and Millie were comfortably installed there opposite Sam, with the fourth seat saved for Philip. Millie found herself in one of the window seats. She stowed her jacket and backpack in the overhead luggage rack and sat down, only to wonder if she'd died and gone to heaven. Because there was Sam, sitting just across the table, and smiling at her again, albeit a little sleepily.

'So, Millie,' he said, leaning forward to reduce the space between them even more. 'First time in Paris?'

This was it, then. Millie couldn't quite believe it. Here she was on a train, on her way to Paris, and sitting right opposite Sam Tulliver, and he was talking, actually *talking* to her, not just saying 'Hi' or asking what room the next class was in. She just hoped the concealer was doing its work properly so he wouldn't notice the spot on her chin. This was turning out to be the best day ever, and not even the unpleasantness with Nate could spoil it now.

But what ought she to say to Sam? How best to impress him?

After an agonising pause, during which she mentally came up with and discarded a whole bunch of replies she sensed were probably not nearly as witty as they seemed, she said, 'Yes.' And then, because instinct told her this wasn't likely to get her very far, added, 'How about you?'

Obviously she must have said the right thing, because Sam carried on talking.

'Sort of. We went through it once on the way to skiing, but there wasn't much time to look around. What are you looking forward to most today? The boat trip?'

Millie was still carefully considering what her reply should be when Paula chipped in with, 'The shops!'

Millie felt a flash of irritation. This was her conversation, dammit. Paula could at least *try* not to hi-jack it. So she quickly added, 'Père Lachaise.'

Paula groaned. 'You see, that's what I don't understand. What's the point of traipsing around a stupid old cemetery? It's full of dead people! Why can't we go shopping instead? At least that would give us a chance to practise our French on live French people. I mean, you can't talk to dead ones.'

Millie saw her opportunity, and grasped it. 'Ah, but they're very *famous* dead people.' She already knew everything there was to know about Père Lachaise, the biggest cemetery in Paris. She had done a virtual tour of it on the official website, and knew exactly which graves she wanted to visit. 'Oscar Wilde is buried there!'

Sam and Paula looked at her blankly. Millie stared back at them in disbelief. Surely they'd heard of Oscar Wilde? She decided it was her duty to educate them.

'He was a celebrated wit and poet and playwright. He wrote *The Importance of Being Earnest*, which is just about the funniest play ever. He was persecuted in London because of his homosexuality and exiled to Paris, where he died in 1900. His last words were, "Either this wallpaper goes or I do".'

This little speech came tumbling out in a rush, and Millie wondered if she was talking too much. But Sam was looking impressed. 'Blimey. How do you know all this?'

'She's such a little nerd,' Paula said, ruffling Millie's hair.

Paula was joking, of course, but Millie didn't much like having her hair ruffled, particularly since she had gone to so much effort to make it lie flat, and she especially didn't like being called a 'little nerd' in front of Sam, even as a joke. She had noticed before that Paula's character sometimes changed when she was talking to boys. Sometimes she even teased Millie in front of them, and although she didn't do it spitefully, like Nate, Millie wished she wouldn't do it at all. It made her feel like Paula's stupid little sister, or one of the faded companions from a Jane Austen novel.

Philip had turned up halfway through Millie's Oscar Wilde speech. He extracted a portable game console before slinging his bag on to the rack and sitting down opposite Paula. 'Père Lachaise cemetery? You know Jim Morrison's buried there as well?'

Millie eyed the console warily, hoping Philip wasn't going to be making bleeping noises all the way to Paris.

But at the mention of Jim Morrison, Sam seemed to wake up. 'You're kidding!' he said with obvious enthusiasm. Now it was clear he was *really* interested, and Millie realised to her disappointment he'd probably only pretended to be impressed by her Oscar Wilde monologue, just to be polite. He probably did think of her as just Paula's nerdy little friend, after all.

'All right, I give up,' said Paula, exaggerating her dumb blonde act, which Millie usually found amusing but which was now beginning to get on her nerves. 'Who's Jim Morrison?'

'Pop singer,' Millie said, trying not to sound too condescending. She couldn't understand how someone as bright as Paula could sometimes be so ignorant, though obviously Paula didn't spend nearly as much time on the internet as Millie. She was too busy living her life in the real world.

'*Rock* singer, please,' said Philip. 'Legendary. Never heard of The Doors?'

'Of course I have,' Millie said, feeling mildly offended, but Philip had been addressing Paula, not her. And naturally Paula pretended to be thrilled when Philip invited her round to his house the next weekend so he could give her a crash course in sixties pop music. Millie tried not to sigh too loudly. How come Philip couldn't see, as she could, that Paula had no interest whatsoever in a bunch of old pop singers she'd never heard of, and that she would probably have squealed with pleasure if he'd offered to play her recordings of humpbacked whales mating?

But Millie was also aware that at least some of her irritation was because she so badly wanted to be included in the invitation, even though there was no way her parents would ever let her go round to the house of someone they hadn't thoroughly vetted, not even with Paula there as chaperone. And Paula would probably want to be on her own with Philip anyway. Millie would just get in the way.

The thought of her dreary, dead-end life was threatening to plunge her into gloom, which it did quite often, but she summoned all her willpower to shrug it off and pull herself together. This was stupid. She was going to Paris! She would have a good time if it killed her!

Everyone cheered as the train began to move, and Millie immediately felt as if a weight had been lifted from her shoulders. She'd done it! She'd escaped! Nothing could stop her now. She was on her way!

Paula knelt up on her seat and peered around the carriage. 'I don't see Nate,' she said, sitting back down again.

Philip let out a low whistle. 'You don't know?'

'Know what?' Paula and Millie and Sam leant forward, all ears, and Philip was clearly thrilled to have found listeners who had to yet hear the news.

'He almost got arrested for shouting about bombs.'

'No!' said Paula.

'Oh yes,' said Philip, enjoying himself. 'All these gorillas appeared out of nowhere and rugby-tackled him to the ground. They put him in handcuffs! Ryan had his work cut out persuading them to let him go, but even then they wouldn't let him get on the train. Ryan was livid and ordered him to go home. He'll probably get detention tomorrow, maybe even expelled.'

The others stared at him in amazement.

'Sheesh,' said Sam. 'I told him not to drink that double espresso.'

Paula flung her arm around Millie's shoulders and ruffled her hair again. 'You see! That's what he gets for messing with our Millie!'

Millie tried to wrap her head around the news that Nate was off the trip. What a fantastic start to the day! Maybe it would turn out to be perfect, after all.

Sam and Philip began to joke about what might have happened to Nate if he had been arrested and gone to jail. Millie had thought they were Nate's friends, but they didn't sound very friendly towards him as they started sniggering about cellmates and tattoos and bending over to retrieve soap in the showers. She suppressed a shudder. Boy humour was sometimes so baffling. How could they find things like that funny?

As the train sped through the dark landscape, Paula and Philip started nattering about which countries they'd already visited (family holidays in France, Portugal and, in Paula's case, Greece and America) and which countries they wanted to visit (which, naturally, was a much longer list) which left the way clear for Sam and Millie to talk uninterrupted.

After a few awkward moments, Millie found herself relaxing, and managed to keep herself from babbling too much useless information. They chatted mostly about music and films, and though Millie always had to wait until films came out on DVD before she could see them (going to the cinema was out of the question, of course), and although she hadn't actually listened to many of the bands Sam was talking about, her voracious reading and internet surfing stood her in good stead, since she knew all sorts of interesting facts about nearly everything he mentioned.

Sam's favourite film was - surprise! - *Star Wars*, which Millie thought was OK but mainly for kids. Of course she didn't say that to Sam, though she did tell him the plot had been based on an old Japanese samurai movie called *The Hidden Fortress*, which Sam had never heard of, but which he now vowed to watch as soon as possible.

But she was disappointed when he told her he hardly ever read books, just the bare minimum they were assigned to study for school. And he'd never even heard of most of Millie's favourite writers. He did like graphic novels and superhero comics, though, so they talked about those for a bit, and the subject turned out to be more interesting than Millie had anticipated. When she asked Sam why superheroes always seemed to be male, he told her about Wonder Woman and Invisible Girl and Jean Grey from X-Men, who turned into Dark Phoenix, and Millie made a mental note to ask Mrs. Crumley to order the comics so she could read them for herself.

Sam also liked computers and read a lot of computer magazines. Millie was grateful for her laptop, which provided her with a vital link to the outside world, but didn't think she could ever get quite so passionate about it as Sam clearly was about his PC.

In fact, the more smoothly their conversation flowed, the more Millie started wondering what had attracted her to Sam in the first place. Surely it couldn't just have been the way he looked? He was one of the most good-natured people she had ever met, that was for sure, and never seemed to take offence at anything, or lose his temper or start arguments. Millie liked that a lot. But most of his opinions seemed to lack conviction or originality, as though he were simply recycling something he'd heard somebody else say.

Millie soon found out, however, that there were two areas where Sam's enthusiasm could not be topped. The first was the rock band he'd formed with Philip, Simon and Dyson; they'd named it Why So Serious, after a line from a Batman movie.

The second area was sport. Any old sport. Football, tennis, golf, rugby, athletics, snooker... Sam didn't care, as long as it involved a ball, or running fast, or jumping over things.

'It's weird,' he said. 'Whenever I've got the ball, it feels as though I *am* the ball, and that somehow I can make it do whatever I want. Sometimes, when I score a goal, it's as though it's *me*, and not the ball, there in the back of the net.'

Millie expressed polite interest, but when he mistook that for encouragement and started to talk about Arsenal, she felt her eyelids beginning to droop and had to concentrate hard to stop them closing altogether.

She was jerked back into wakefulness by a voice from the public address system. The train was approaching the Channel Tunnel.

The announcement was greeted in the carriage by a ripple of excitement. Millie knew Paula and Philip had already taken the shuttle with their families, but for her and many others this was the first time they'd been out of the country. Some of the boys made jokes about the train getting stuck in the tunnel and the sea bursting through the walls and flooding the carriage. Millie overheard Marley Finnegan telling Sissy Urquhart, 'We'll all have to hold our breath and swim!' which was wicked of him since everybody knew Sissy was scared of water.

But then the train passed into the tunnel and the view from the windows became impenetrably dark, and Millie forgot about Sam and Paula and Philip and Marley and Sissy and everybody else, because she began to feel a little strange.

It started with a flutter in the pit of her stomach, which at first she dismissed as nerves, and not just about being 130 to 250 feet below sea level. For the first time in her life she was leaving the country, and she'd had to lie to her parents to do it. And then there had been the upsetting scene with Nate, and on top of that she was talking to Sam. *Sam!* So it was only natural that her stomach should be playing up, the way it played up before she had to read something out loud to the rest of the class, or that time she'd auditioned for a school play. (Thanks to her scowl, she had landed the plum role of the Wicked Witch of the West in a production of *The Wizard of Oz*, but her parents had forced her to pull out since it would have meant attending evening rehearsals.)

After ten minutes, the feeling in her stomach began to change, and not for the better. It was getting stronger. To begin with, it had felt like butterflies, but now it was as though she had a miniature Loch Ness monster trapped inside her. And the monster was thrashing around, trying to force its way up through her throat and out of her mouth into the carriage.

Millie started to panic. What if she threw up? Right here, right in front of everyone? Right in front of Sam? Oh lord, what if she threw up *on* Sam? Please don't let that happen, she prayed. Anything but that. It would be the worst thing in the world. She would be completely and utterly humiliated. She would have to leave Mallory Hall and go to another school, because there would be no way she could face anyone ever again.

She was vaguely aware of Sam saying something, but all she could do was sit there, frozen with fear, trying to distract herself from the awful interior churning by thinking about the Mona Lisa and the River Seine and Père Lachaise cemetery, and all the other things she'd been looking forward to seeing once they got to Paris.

But it was hard to think of anything when there was a type of dreary hymn running through her head, over and over again, and though she couldn't identify the tune itself, it reminded her of the Bramblewood villagers singing in the pub. But darker, and more ominous.

On another level of consciousness, she could still hear Sam going on about Arsenal, and Paula was saying idiotic things about a pop star she fancied, but their voices were faint and fuzzy now, as though someone had wrapped a thick blanket of cotton wool around Millie's head.

She realised that if she really was going to vomit, she would have to get to the toilets as soon as possible, but she couldn't summon the words to ask Paula to let her squeeze past into the aisle, and she wasn't sure she had the strength to make it as far as the end of the carriage anyway. Her limbs felt too heavy to move.

So she stayed where she was, trying not to hyperventilate, and screwed her eyes shut and told herself that, whatever this was, it would soon be over.

But it wasn't over, not by a long chalk. Pretty soon she felt a throbbing in her head, ten times worse than any headache she could remember.

And this wasn't a headache, she realised with an awareness so acute it only added to the pain.

This was something worse.

Chapter 4
Code Crimson

'Millie? Millie? Millie!'

Through the cotton wool, she could hear Paula saying her name over and over again.

'Millie? Are you OK?'

And someone else, probably Philip, saying, 'Turn her head to one side,' and someone else was saying, 'I'll get Fletcher.'

But it was hard to distinguish these voices from the other ones in her head, which were not just singing now, but chanting, in a language that wasn't English, and which didn't sound much like French either.

And then Millie opened her eyes, and the train carriage was gone, and Paula and Sam and Philip and everyone else with it.

All she could see was red. Her brain felt like a piece of expanding elastic that was being stretched tighter, tighter, tighter until suddenly, just before she thought her head would explode, something inside her gave way with a dull ping, and something else snapped back into place with a loud twang, and she heard another sound like a thousand people sighing in unison, and then her head was full of innumerable other strange voices, crying and sobbing and screaming and laughing all at once, and in the centre of it a still, small voice that she somehow recognised as her own was saying, 'They *know*.

They know I'm here,' though for the life of her she couldn't have said who *they* were, or how *they* knew, or exactly where *here* was.

Then she couldn't hear the sobbing and screaming any more - just laughter. It was horrible laughter, vicious and cruel, and her head was full of it. And she knew without a shadow of a doubt, and with an overwhelming feeling of guilt, that she had just made someone evil very, very happy.

And then, just like that, the pain disappeared, and with it the headache and the laughter. It was like the feeling of relief when her sinuses were all bunged up after a heavy cold but then her ears popped and her head was instantly clear again.

Something brushed her cheek and she swatted it away. She heard somebody saying, 'Quick, her nose is bleeding,' and opened her eyes.

The armrest separating her seat from Paula's had been folded up and she was lying across both seats with her legs dangling into the aisle. Mrs. Fletcher was crouched over her with a frozen expression like a squirrel caught in headlights. She was dabbing at Millie's nose with a red-blotched paper tissue.

Lined up behind her was what appeared to be the whole of Millie's class. Some, like Paula, looked concerned, others frightened or simply curious. One or two seemed enthralled, which Millie thought was inappropriate. Did they think this was a circus? She felt mortified.

But it wasn't quite the end of the world, because she hadn't thrown up. At least, she didn't think so.

'I'm all right.'

She struggled to sit up, which wasn't easy with Mrs. Fletcher half on top of her. Some of the onlookers drifted away. Alison Moseby actually looked disappointed that Millie wasn't seriously ill or dying. Mrs. Fletcher, on the other hand, was beaming as though someone had just handed her the best birthday present in the world. 'You had me worried there, Millie. You should have told us you had epilepsy.'

'I don't,' Millie said, but didn't press the point. She knew she had to stay calm. She'd only just left England. The last thing she wanted was to be sent home now. 'I just fainted, I think. Probably because I got up so early and skipped breakfast. But I'm all right now, really I am.'

'You can go back to your seats,' Paula said, flapping her arms at the remaining gawkers. 'Go on, shoo! Leave us alone.'

'Nothing to see here,' said Sam. 'Off you go.'

The combined social clout of Sam and Paula was enough to send the stragglers back to their seats, though even from where Millie was lying she could hear Bonetta Reese muttering, 'Bloody drama queen. First Nate, now this. Absolutely *has* to be the centre of attention.'

'Are you sure you're OK?' Mrs. Fletcher asked as she stood up. 'We can get the train to stop at Calais...'

'I'm fine, really I am,' Millie repeated. And she really was, she realised. The headache was barely even a memory now, and the only flutter in her stomach was of regular excitement.

'Well, if you're sure,' Mrs. Fletcher said doubtfully as she backed slowly away. 'I guess it might have been the cabin pressure or something.'

'Something like that,' Millie said, smiling brightly, though not too brightly, because she didn't want Mrs.

Fletcher thinking she was deranged on top of everything else.

'She'll be OK,' said Paula, waving the teacher on her way. 'Don't worry, I'll keep an eye on her. The minute she starts frothing at the mouth and rolling around on the floor in convulsions I'll let you know.'

Mrs. Fletcher went back to her seat, wearing an expression that suggested it had been she, rather than Millie, who had just recovered from a medical emergency.

Not that Millie had any idea about what had just happened. The odd thing was that even the memory of it was now fading, leaving her with only the faintest of disagreeable impressions, as though it was something unpleasant that had happened to her in a dream.

A bad dream. Like the one with the bats. That was all it had been.

'Was I really convulsing?' she asked Paula.

'No, you just went all floppy. Kind of cute, actually.'

'We could see the whites of your eyes,' said Philip. 'It was better than *The Evil Dead*.'

'Oh God, I'm so embarrassed.' Millie dabbed at her nostrils with the paper tissue Mrs. Fletcher had left, but the bleeding had stopped.

'No shame in feeling ill,' said Sam. 'Happens to the best of us. Hey Phil, remember when Dickie Manning caught one right in the nuts in the Trinity match?'

'He went green and projectile vomited over the linesman,' said Philip.

Millie was grateful to them for trying to make her feel better. 'Well, at least I didn't throw up,' she said, before adding anxiously, 'I didn't throw up, did I?'

'You did *not* throw up,' Paula confirmed.

She ruffled Millie's hair again, but this time Millie didn't mind. Most of it had escaped from the ponytail anyway, so she would have to find a mirror and tie it all back again. She hoped it didn't look like an explosion in a mattress factory, but then decided she didn't care either way. There were things more important than well-behaved hair.

'You showed admirable restraint,' Paula was saying. 'We're proud of you, kiddo.'

'Bloody hell,' Millie sighed. 'What a day.'

'And it's only just begun!' Paula patted her on the shoulder and pointed to the window. Millie looked round and saw flat countryside flashing by in the palest of early morning daylight. It didn't look much different from the England they'd left behind, and yet...

Millie stared, mesmerised. 'Is that...?'

'Yep,' said Sam. 'We're in France now.'

*****

It was the end of an exhausting night. Miss Pim had been exceptionally demanding. With a heavy sigh, Dupontel settled back into the capacious white leather sofa, plumped his stockinged feet on the matching white leather footstool in front of him, and stroked the white cat napping next to him. He knew that Miss Pim's sometimes excruciating perfectionism was just one of the reasons why she was running a fashion empire, while he, Dupontel, was just one of her minions, required to hover at her elbow at all times, prepared to act on her every whim, however unreasonable.

But honestly, did she have to be *quite* so bossy?

He inhaled the heady bouquet rising from his amber-coloured Extra Old, and took a sip, slooshing the aromatic liquid warmth around his mouth before allowing it to slither down his gullet. A small measure of Armagnac just before bedtime was one of the few indulgences he permitted himself. That, and a single cigarette per day. After all, he wouldn't want to be in anything but peak physical condition when the time came for him to claim his big reward. What was the point of living for ever if you were trapped in a substandard body with wrinkly skin and a beer belly? Once he'd been turned into a vampire, he would be able to smoke and drink to his heart's content, secure in the knowledge that his youth and beauty would never fade.

And he was good-looking, dazzlingly so. Everyone told him that. Until the big day, though, it was a question of discipline, and of unquestioningly doing all that was required of him. And if he sometimes felt as though he were being treated like a servant, that was OK. As soon as he was a vampire, he too would have minions of his own to boss around.

With his free hand, Dupontel loosened his tie and starched collar, which had left an angry red mark on his neck. Miss Pim insisted her staff dress formally at all times, but Dupontel was already toying with the idea of introducing a more casual dress code as soon as he was in a position of authority. Trainers perhaps, and jeans - though of course they would have to be *designer* trainers and *designer* jeans, and preferably from Maison Pim.

But that was still in the future. Right now, as always, he was looking forward to blotting out the rising sun with his custom-made light-tight curtains, climbing into bed and slipping into a deep and dreamless sleep.

With luck, he would get five or six hours before it was time to wake up again and attend to the afternoon's business.

So he did not feel kindly disposed towards the telephone when it rang.

It was an old-fashioned telephone, gleaming white to match the rest of the spotless decor, and Dupontel knew only too well that it was used only in cases of direst emergency. What was it now, he wondered irritably. Another high-ranking politician to be bought off? Clementine making a spectacle of herself in public again? Or the discreet disposal of an inconvenient corpse? He sighed and picked up the receiver.

In another second he was sitting bolt upright, wide-awake, the glass of Armagnac forgotten.

The caller uttered only two words, but they were enough to prod him into full wakefulness.

'Code Crimson.'

The line abruptly went dead.

Propelled by a surge of adrenalin, Dupontel leapt to his feet, crossed to the dozing computer and tapped in a code known only to him and a select few others. He stared at the screen as it sprang to life, and felt the hairs on the back of his neck prickle to attention.

According to the data, the seal had been broken at 07h43, Central European Time.

He swore as he picked up his portable phone, tapped out a three-digit number, and asked to be put through to Watch Duty.

'Dupontel!' Dupontel recognised the voice of Olivier Poiret. 'Long time, no see. So you've heard the news? What's happening? Where are you? This is exciting, isn't it!'

Dupontel couldn't be bothered with small talk. 'Point of entry?'

There was some humming and hawing on the other end of the line. Then, 'According to our calculations, it was almost certainly the Eurostar that got into the Gare du Nord at 08h50. Passenger list on its way to you even as we speak.'

'Good God, man. That was over an hour ago!' Dupontel couldn't hide his irritation. 'What took you so long? We should have been there to meet it!'

'All right, all right, keep your hair on,' muttered Poiret. 'There was a bit of a mix-up with the monitoring equipment. The flood prevention alarm was going off, and by the time we traced the problem back to its source the train was already in... Of course, it would help if we knew what we were looking for. Can't we ask the Syndicate for more information?'

'Duh,' said Dupontel, thinking not for the first time that Poiret was a moron. 'You know they can't be reached until nightfall.'

'Yes, but in an emergency like this...?'

'You want to be the idiot who wakes them up?' snapped Dupontel. Waking an executive officer during the day was out of the question, since it would very likely end with loss of life. Specifically the life of whoever was foolish enough to be doing the waking.

Dupontel would have to deal with this on his own. He felt excitement welling up inside him, and more than a little anxiety as well. This was his big chance. If he pulled this off, Miss Pim would surely decide it was time for his long overdue promotion.

And if he screwed up? No, it didn't bear thinking about. All he had to do was keep a cool head.

'What do the initial stats say?' he asked in what he hoped was a cool, measured tone rather than an overeager, panicky one.

There was a papery rustling at the other end of the line, as though Poiret were shuffling through a stack of printouts. Dupontel tried to swallow his impatience. At long last, Poiret started muttering again, like an absent-minded professor talking to himself.

'Party of British and American physicists, in town for a symposium at La Villette... Rugby team from King's College, Cambridge... Oh! A group of fifteen women, booked into the Hotel Baudelaire for what seems to be... yes, a hen party! One of them's getting married at the weekend...'

'Too old,' said Dupontel. 'For heaven's sake, man, we're looking for someone in a lower age bracket. Sixteen, tops. Didn't you read the memo?'

'We've had stacks of memos over the years,' Poiret reminded him. 'All this paperwork, you know it's not always easy to keep track... No, wait... There's a party of schoolchildren here. From Mallory Hall, in Kent, which is a *département* near...'

'I know where Kent is,' said Dupontel.

'Are we looking for a male or a female?' asked Poiret.

Dupontel didn't answer the question, because he didn't know. 'How old are these schoolchildren?'

'Fifth form, according to this,' said Poiret. 'But that's the old English school system, so let's see, that would make them...'

'Fifteen or sixteen!' said Dupontel, feeling his heart beat faster. 'That's the one. That *has* to be the one. Get someone out there, right now! Put some Watchers on their tail.'

After more papery rustling, Poiret said, 'According to this, they're booked on a train back to London tonight.'

'Then there's no time to lose, is there,' Dupontel said in his haughtiest manner. 'Are all the alerts in place and primed?'

'Of course!' Poiret sounded faintly hurt. 'But wait...' He dragged the pause out for longer than was necessary, as though to punish Dupontel for his harsh tone.

Dupontel tried to swallow his impatience. 'Well?'

'One of them's going off right now!'

Dupontel craned forward, as though trying to hear the alarm down the phone. 'Which one? Where?'

He could hear Poiret breathing heavily, and a faint clicking as he typed something on his keyboard. Then his voice came back on the line.

'Greek Antiquities.'

A slow smile spread across Dupontel's face. This was going to be easy.

'They're in the Louvre!'

Chapter 5
Oysters

'What's the matter, Mill? You look as though you've seen a ghost.'

Much to Millie's annoyance, Sam had taken to knocking the last syllable off her name. But she laughed nervously and shook her head. 'Just a bit tired.'

'It's only a naked man, Millie,' said Paula. 'But he is rather cute, isn't he?'

Millie decided it probably was just fatigue that had made her think she'd seen the statue move. And after the face-off with Nate and her dizzy spell on the train, the last thing she needed was to make another scene. Everyone would think she was going bonkers.

But for an instant, as she'd been walking past the statue, she could have sworn she'd seen the head swivel, and the marble eyes fixing their empty gaze on her.

She immediately turned back for another, longer look, mainly just to reassure herself that she'd been imagining things. It was the statue of a young Greek gladiator, which had already attracted no small amount of attention from her fellow pupils because he wasn't wearing any clothes.

The figure was leaning forward, weight on its right leg, with the left arm thrust into the air, a pose that displayed the young man's muscled physique to perfection and incidentally provided an excuse for some of her classmates to exercise their unsophisticated wit, or giggle hysterically.

But Millie wasn't studying the statue's anatomy; she was watching the head intently, daring it to move again, although the more she stared, the more inanimate it seemed. It was only when she was looking at something else, with the gladiator relegated to the corner of her eye, that she had the impression it wasn't as solid as it appeared. But how could the statue move? The very idea was ridiculous. It was made of marble.

Miss Brown was trying to chivvy them along. 'Gratified as I am to see you all taking such an interest in classical sculpture, may I remind you that we have a schedule to keep. Let's go, people!'

Millie was happy to turn her back on the gladiator and scurry after Mr. Ryan as he led the way towards a wide marble staircase dominated by another marble statue, a huge one with wings. No problem there, Millie thought as she looked up at it. This one couldn't possibly be watching her, because it didn't have a head.

Her relief was short-lived. As she followed the others through a long gallery lined with paintings, she found herself becoming increasingly twitchy. It was like the gladiator statue all over again. With nearly every step she thought she glimpsed movement in the pictures, but when she turned to face them full on, they were just old paintings, and resolutely two-dimensional. Though she did wonder why quite so *many* of them were showing the severed head of John the Baptist.

Here it was, on a plate, its eyes firmly closed, though she'd had the distinct impression, only a moment ago, that it had been looking at her. And here it was again, being dangled by the hair in front of a beautiful woman who didn't seem the slightest bit discomfited at being presented with such a gory trophy. Millie concluded the woman was Salome, who according to the Bible demanded the Baptist's head as a reward for dancing The Dance of the Seven Veils for her stepfather, Herod. Oscar Wilde had written a play about it.

But the head didn't seem too bothered at having been separated from the rest of its body. In fact, it was looking at Millie quite calmly, even though she could have sworn that only a moment ago its eyes had been closed.

She turned away with a shudder and hurried to catch up with the rest of the group, which was now passing into a part of the gallery where the walls were painted blood red. Everyone was clustered in front of a massive dark canvas showing a bunch of semi-naked people sprawled on top of one another in front of a storm-tossed sea. Mrs. Fletcher was telling them about the painting's history; it was called The Raft of the Medusa, and had been inspired by a real-life shipwreck in which over a hundred people had been set adrift on a small raft, where they'd all gone mad and started eating each other.

'God, this is boring,' said Paula, stifling a yawn.

'I think it's pretty cool,' said Philip. 'Did you hear what Fletch just said? The artist used real corpses as models!'

'I don't mean the painting,' Paula said hastily, not wanting to disagree. 'I just think we'd get more practice speaking French if we went to a market. Or maybe a department store.'

Millie didn't say anything. She felt overwhelmed by the painting, which seemed to be swallowing her up. The waves looked so realistic she could almost feel the ground heave beneath her feet. She put out a hand to steady herself against one of the blood red walls, but quickly removed it when she saw one of the museum guards glaring in her direction.

The skin of the people on the raft was a livid greenish colour, but not all of them were dead - she could see that now, because one or two had shifted position. And one of them was pointing straight at her...

'Millie!'

Millie jumped. Mrs. Fletcher was standing right behind her. 'No more fainting fits, I hope?'

'I'm fine,' said Millie, though in reality she was feeling a little seasick.

'Impressive, isn't it.' Mrs. Fletcher nodded at the canvas. 'It's one of my favourites. The painter's name is Théodore Géricault.' She pronounced the name slowly and clearly.

'It's disturbing,' said Millie, eyeing the painting warily. She was relieved to see the figure no longer seemed to be pointing at her, but rather at something in the distance, possibly a ship. She grimaced and said, 'Why couldn't he have painted pretty flowers and kittens and things, like normal well-adjusted people?'

Mrs. Fletcher laughed and patted her on the shoulder. 'Then it wouldn't be art, would it. It would a picture on the lid of a box of chocolates. Come along now, it's time for the Big One. I expect you've heard of the movie *The Da Vinci Code*?'

Millie nodded and told Mrs. Fletcher she'd read the novel. In truth she'd found it was not to her taste and had stopped reading after a hundred pages, but she wasn't sorry to have an excuse to leave the The Raft of the Medusa behind. She scurried to catch up with Mr. Ryan, who was leading his pupils through a doorway up ahead.

Thanks to the early hour, the galleries had seemed relatively empty up until now, but this smaller room was already thronged with so many people that at first, Millie couldn't see what they were looking at, especially with her eyeline blocked by so many arms holding up mobile phones to take snaps.

Then, through the thicket of heads and phones, she glimpsed a sheet of thick glass on the far wall, a dark painting just visible beneath it. It was the portrait of a woman smiling enigmatically. Millie recognised her instantly: Mona Lisa, by Leonardo da Vinci.

Esther Filbert said loudly, 'I thought it would be bigger.'

'Is that it?' Paula was unimpressed. '*That's* what we've come all this way to see?'

Mr. Ryan heard her. 'We couldn't let you go back without seeing the Mona Lisa now could we? It's the most famous painting in the world!'

'I want my money back,' said Paula, and she was only half joking.

Millie stood on tiptoe to try and get a better view over the sea of heads. She too was a little disappointed. The painting was so very small and dark, and the Mona Lisa herself looked rather ordinary.

Except for the eyes, Millie saw now. Even from a distance, they looked unnervingly realistic. It was as though Leonardo had used some early form of holographic technology. The eyes moved from side to side and finally came to rest on Millie, who let out a squeal and stumbled backwards. One or two people looked round to see what she was squealing at, but evidently concluded she had simply tripped over somebody's feet.

Sam caught her by the arm to help her recover her balance. 'Are you sure you're all right? You're still looking awfully pale.

'I don't know,' Millie admitted. 'It's a bit much, seeing all these pictures like this, all at once. It's kind of... overpowering.'

Sam looked intrigued. 'I once saw a horror movie about a woman who fainted in an art gallery and dreamt she was actually *inside* the paintings.'

'Well, I'm not inside them,' Millie explained. 'It's just that some of them seem so... real. It's like the eyes are following me around, you know?'

She immediately regretted having said that, but Sam didn't laugh. He seemed genuinely interested. 'I know what you mean. Some of them are a bit creepy, aren't they?'

'It's almost as though they know I'm here,' said Millie. 'And it's probably because I'm so tired, but... I keep thinking I can see them moving.'

'Like the portraits in the Harry Potter movies?' said Sam.

Millie nodded, grateful that he wasn't taking the mickey out of her. 'Exactly! But at least they're not talking to me as well, like the Harry Potter ones. That would be *really* creepy.'

'You're right,' Sam said gravely. 'That would be really serious. I'd have to start worrying about you then.'

Millie was deciding she rather liked the idea of Sam worrying about her, but they were interrupted by Paula complaining she was hungry. 'When's lunch?'

Sam checked his watch. 'Not for a couple of hours.'

'I'll die of starvation.'

'Like those poor sods on the raft,' Philip chipped in. 'You're going to end up chowing down on the rest of us.'

Paula slipped her arm through Sam's. 'Didn't you have an extra Mars Bar? Don't deny it, now.'

'I did indeed,' said Sam. He fished the chocolate bar out of his pocket and handed it to Paula, who wolfed it down in a couple of bites. Millie glanced over towards one of the museum guards. Surely it was against the rules to eat in the Louvre? But no one seemed to have noticed.

The crowd between Millie and the Mona Lisa wasn't growing any thinner. In fact, there seemed to be more people than ever craning their necks, trying to get a glimpse of the painting and taking photos of it, presumably as proof they'd seen it, though Millie wondered why they didn't just buy a postcard from the gift shop.

'OK, that's it,' said Mr. Ryan. 'Follow me, people.' And he turned to lead the way out.

As she was leaving, Millie risked one more glance over her shoulder at the painting. And immediately wished she hadn't.

The Mona Lisa seemed almost to be winking at her.

*****

Millie had been nervous about the boat trip, because she had never been in a boat before and feared she might be seasick. Her experience with The Raft of the Medusa hadn't exactly been reassuring. If even a painted ocean could make her feel queasy, she fretted, what might happen once she found herself on a *real* boat, in the middle of the River Seine, at the mercy of the elements?

But to her surprise, the boat trip turned out to be the most stress-free leg of the trip so far. The initial feverish excitement at being in Paris had worn off, leaving her calm and curious and eager to see as much of the city as she could. The odd things she'd glimpsed in the Louvre had obviously been the result of her sleep-deprived eyes playing tricks on her brain. The paintings hadn't really been moving. Of course they hadn't. Paintings didn't move.

She chuckled inwardly at her own foolishness. Thank goodness she'd managed not to make a fuss. Perhaps she'd said too much to Sam, but he'd taken it in his stride and seemed now to have forgotten about it.

She'd been hoping to find herself seated next to Sam on the boat, but Paula had somehow ended up wedged between them and was now whispering intently into his ear, leaving Millie sandwiched between Paula and Philip. Millie didn't mind, but she could tell Philip was miffed at having lost his spot next to Paula, and she couldn't help wondering what Paula might be saying to Sam that was so urgent, and so very private.

The sun had finally pushed through the grey clouds, but its light was watery, without warmth, and there was a stiff breeze, so Millie was glad of the plexiglass canopy sheltering the deck. She thought it might also be a safety measure, to prevent reckless passengers from clowning around and falling overboard. There would always be at least one idiot who would try to impress his pals by hanging off the rail. Millie looked around at the other pupils; yes, it was precisely the sort of thing Marley Finnegan or Russell Jones would do, given the chance.

But, canopy or no canopy, as they chugged out into the river the view of both banks was spectacular.

Over the noise of the engines and the excited chatter of her classmates, Millie thought she could hear shouting. She looked back at the jetty they'd just left, and saw half a dozen smartly dressed men and women lined up along the water's edge, flapping their arms quite comically, as though they wanted the boat to turn back and pick them up. Perhaps they were late for an important lunch date.

They'll fall in if they don't watch out, Millie thought before redirecting her attention to The Statue of Liberty up ahead.

'I thought the Statue of Liberty was in New York,' said Coral Baines. Miss Brown told them *this* Statue of Liberty was a quarter-scale replica of the full-sized one, which had been presented to America by the people of France in 1886 to commemorate the hundred-year anniversary of the signing of the Declaration of Independence.

It was the perfect way to see Paris. The boat chugged past the Eiffel Tower, and the Zouave statue on the Pont de l'Alma, which Parisians used to gauge rising flood levels, and the beautiful Musée d'Orsay, which had once been a railway station but was now an art gallery. They passed the Louvre, which seemed almost like an old friend now, and the Île de la Cité in the middle of the river.

Millie thought the buildings on the island looked quite forbidding - especially the Conciergerie, where Marie Antoinette had been imprisoned before her execution - but she was thrilled when the boat looped around the next island, the much friendlier-looking Île Saint-Louis, and she was finally able to get a good look at Notre-Dame cathedral, about which she'd read so much.

As if on cue, while the boat was chugging past the cathedral the bells began to ring. Stu Barker and Brian Erskine started doing hunchback impressions, and only when Brian actually tried to lift Sissy Urquhart out of her seat and run up and down the aisle with her did Mr. Ryan put a stop to their grotesque capering.

Millie could happily have spent all day chugging up and down the river, but all too soon the boat was pulling up at another jetty, and the pupils were herded back on to the waiting bus, to be taken to what the schedule had promised would be 'lunch in a typical Parisian brasserie.'

'About time too,' said Paula as they found their seats on the bus. 'I'm so hungry I could eat a horse.'

'You might be able to,' said Millie. ''The French eat horses.'

'And snails. And frogs' legs,' said Philip.

'At least they don't eat dogs, like in Korea!' said Sam. He caught sight of Paula's face and added, 'Only joking, Paula. They don't really eat dogs there.'

'But there do seem to be an awful lot of dogs in Paris,' said Philip. 'Listen, can't you hear them?'

Now that he mentioned it, Millie realised he was right. She couldn't *see* any dogs, but when she tried to blot out the thrum of the bus engine, her ears picked up a faint clamour of distant barking. She wondered what on earth could be making the dogs bark like that.

Perhaps they were passing messages to one another, she thought, like the dogs in *101 Dalmatians.*

*****

Horse wasn't on the menu. The brasserie was already busy, but the school had reserved places, and some of the tables had been pulled together so they could sit together in three groups.

Millie studied the menu and smiled to herself. When a waiter came round to take their orders, Paula and Sam, like most of the others, opted for steak and chips, which they ordered in self-conscious French, while the teachers looked on and smiled encouragingly. Andrew Quigley and Ayesha Washington were vegetarians and ordered omelettes. A couple of the girls were on diets and asked for salads. Philip was a little more adventurous and ordered duck.

Then it was Millie's turn. She'd been thinking about this a lot, and knew exactly what she wanted. 'Oysters,' she said. Then repeated it in French. *'Les huîtres, s'il vous plaît.'*

The waiter nodded and jotted the order down. Millie's fellow diners weren't quite as sanguine.

'Millie! You've got to be kidding!' said Paula.

'Oysters, Millie?' said Miss Brown from the head of their table. 'Are you sure?'

Bonetta Reese stuck two fingers in her mouth and pretended to vomit. Only Sam was looking at her with fresh respect. 'That's very daring, Millie. Wish I'd thought of it.'

'You could always change your order,' said Millie, inclining her head towards the waiter, who had moved only as far as the next table. But Sam didn't seem in a hurry to cancel his steak and chips.

'I've always wanted to try oysters,' she explained to the rest of the table. 'We don't get them in Bramblewood.'

'My dear,' said Paula, 'you don't get monkey brains in Bramblewood either, but that doesn't mean you've actually got to *eat* the wretched things.'

'Anyway, there's an R in the month,' said Bonetta. 'Which means you shouldn't be eating them.'

'You've got it the wrong way round,' said Millie. 'It's when there *isn't* an R in the month that you shouldn't eat them: May, June, July, August. Don't eat oysters in summer, in other words. It's only logical; they're more likely to be off in hot weather.'

'Whatever,' said Bonetta. 'Go ahead and have your oysters, Miss know-it-all. We all know you'll do anything for attention, even if it makes you sick again.'

'That's enough, Bonetta,' said Miss Brown. 'If Millie wants to try oysters, then she should go ahead and try them. I just hope you know what you're doing, Millie. I'm allergic to them myself.' She smiled apologetically.

For a brief instant, Millie wondered if she was making a huge mistake. She didn't want to spoil the day by being ill again. Then again, she reasoned, if she didn't try oysters now, when would she ever get another chance? Her mother was never going to serve them for lunch, that was for sure.

She was distracted from her thoughts by a hubbub behind her, and looked round. All thoughts of oysters were immediately driven out of her head as she saw Mr. Ryan had got to his feet, and was speaking urgently to a new arrival. Millie couldn't believe her eyes.

Nate McIntyre.

Nate spotted Millie looking at him and scowled back at her, but then Mr. Ryan said something that reclaimed his attention, and he stared down at his shoes and nodded sheepishly. Millie could tell Mr. Ryan was still angry with Nate, but trying not to show it. He was speaking rapidly, and so quietly that no one but Nate could hear what he was saying, but Millie guessed he was telling Nate he'd better be on his best behaviour, or else.

'Well, I wasn't expecting to see *him* again today,' said Paula. 'Must have caught a later train.'

'Boy, he must have *really* wanted to come if he shelled out for another ticket,' said Philip.

'Where did he get the money?' asked Paula. 'Do you think he stole it?'

'I don't care,' said Millie. 'Just as long as he keeps out my way.'

She didn't think Nate would dare make another scene, but she was sorry he had turned up again. He was like a wad of chewing gum stuck to the bottom of her shoe; she just couldn't seem to get rid of him.

As Mr. Ryan finished what he had to say, Nate turned and made a move towards Millie's table, like a dog let off the leash, but Mr. Ryan grabbed him by the collar and firmly indicated the seat next to his own, forcing Brian Erskine to move along to make room. Reluctantly, Nate sat down in the designated chair. But he kept glancing over to the next table, where Millie was sitting.

Bonetta grinned spitefully and said, 'Hey Millie, your boyfriend's back!' She was becoming almost as annoying as Nate.

Paula told Bonetta to get lost, and changed the subject. 'Do you think the waiter was flirting with me?'

'Absolutely not!' said Chandra King. 'He was flirting with *me*.'

'He's not bad-looking,' said Paula, watching as the waiter headed towards the back of the restaurant and pushed through the swing-doors leading to the kitchen. He and his colleagues were clad in smart black suits and long white aprons, and had the astonishing ability to carry six plates, a couple of water jugs and three baskets of bread all at once.

'I think he's just professionally charming,' said Millie.

'Professionally smarmy, if you ask me,' said Ben Drysdale, helping himself to bread. 'French guys really fancy themselves.'

'And with good reason,' said Chandra. 'You can tell they like women.'

'*I* like women,' Ben said with a dirty snigger. 'I *really* like women.'

'That's not what I meant,' said Chandra, looking at him disdainfully.

The restaurant was now full. Waiters were gliding around, depositing large plates of food in front of diners. Millie was captivated, and tuned out of the conversation around her to watch what was going on. She was sitting in a real Parisian brasserie! The air was filled with a delicious smell of coffee and sautéed meat. The room echoed with the comforting clatter of plates and cutlery intermixed with the murmur of conversation from the diners. The waiters seemed instinctively to know what they were doing without anyone having to boss them around. Everything was functioning like clockwork.

Partly from curiosity, and partly to put her schoolgirl French to the test, Millie tried to shut out the noises around her so she could concentrate on what the smartly dressed French couple seated at a table to her left were saying. They were talking too quickly and quietly for her to understand everything, though she did manage to catch the odd word. Someone, she thought it sounded like *Dupontel*, was a complete idiot. Someone else was waiting for permission to do something.

Millie observed the woman covertly. She was extremely beautiful, impossibly thin and effortlessly chic - exactly as Millie had imagined Parisian women would be, though her attire was a little more formal than might have been expected for the hour of day. She was dressed in a cocktail gown made of shimmering silver fabric, with straps as fine as dental floss, and a mink jacket draped over her otherwise exposed shoulders.

The woman kept putting the conversation with her fellow diner on hold so she could talk urgently into her mobile phone. Neither she nor her companion, who was dressed in an incongruously formal tuxedo with a bow tie, seemed terribly interested in the plates on the table in front of them. No wonder she's so skinny, Millie thought enviously. Imagine having a big helping of delicious food like that, right under your nose, and then not touching it.

She wondered if the two diners were having an affair, but eventually concluded their behaviour was more like that of business colleagues than of lovers.

The woman beckoned to one of the waiters, who stopped handing out baskets of bread and hurried over to her. As he leant down to hear what she had to say, he caught sight of Millie watching them, and interrupted the woman to say something in his turn. Millie was amused when she slapped his face - though it was technically more of a pat than a slap - to regain his full attention. How delightfully French, Millie thought.

Just then, though, she lost interest in the altercation, because a huge platter of oysters was being set down in front of her.

'Crikey, you're brave,' said Philip.

'More like stupid,' said Paula. 'No, I didn't mean that, Millie. Go on, tuck in.'

Everyone at the table was watching Millie, who stared at her plate, wondering how to proceed. Someone in the kitchen had already opened the shells, but the oysters inside looked very runny, and very raw.

'The time has come, the walrus said,' said Philip.

'Yeeuch,' said Bonetta. 'They look like foetuses.'

'Shut up,' said Paula.

'They look like snot,' said Chandra.

'Try putting lemon juice on it,' said Sam. 'That's what my mum always does. And then, you sort of loosen it up with the fork.'

Millie picked up one of the wedges of lemon from the side of her plate, and, urged on by Sam, squeezed juice over the nearest mollusc before carefully prising it free of its mooring with her fork.

'Well, here goes.' She raised the half-shell, tipped her head back and let the oyster slide into her mouth. It tasted of cold seawater, and quite slimy, but she had to admit the sensation as it slithered down her throat wasn't entirely unpleasant.

There was a smattering of applause from all her immediate neighbours except Bonetta, who made a face and said 'Yeeuch' again.

'Bravo,' Paula said to Millie. 'Now if you'll excuse me I'm going to eat my steak like a normal person.'

Millie quickly got the hang of oyster-eating and was soon polishing them off like an expert, alternating lemon juice with vinaigrette sauce. She slurped the oysters down until only one remained untouched on the platter, surrounded by the empty shells of its fellows. But this last oyster was larger and, she noticed to her consternation, hadn't fully opened like the others. She tapped it with her fork.

The shell closed, and she jerked back in horror.

'Oh my God! It's still alive!'

Paula let out such a shriek that heads swivelled in their direction.

Sam was unfazed. 'That's normal. It just means it's very fresh, which is good. Look, you stick your knife in that part, and then slide it round, and it should open again. The shell's rough, so watch your fingers.'

Thank goodness Sam was there. Millie followed his instructions, and gazed fascinated as the shell opened up again with a small pop. Instead of slurping up what was inside, though, she could only stare at it, not really understanding what she was seeing. Nestling in the greyish-yellow meat of the last oyster was an object resembling a child's marble, about a quarter of an inch in circumference. At first Millie thought it was dark red, but when she moved her head she saw it was iridescent green. It looked perfectly spherical until she tried to pick it up, when she found it was not smooth at all, but lumpy and misshapen, like two small spheres fused together.

'Oh,' she said, slightly embarrassed. 'I'm not sure this is meant to be here.'

'Ugh,' Paula said, peering at her plate. 'How revolting. You should send it back.'

'What's the problem?' asked Miss Brown. She got to her feet and came over to see what the fuss was about. Her eyes opened wide. 'I don't believe it!'

'Blimey,' said Sam. 'That's a pearl!'

'Are you sure?' asked Paula. 'I thought pearls were, well, pearl-coloured. And round. That thing's all wonky.'

'I once read they come in several different colours.' Millie inclined her head, intrigued by the way the hue changed according to the angle you were looking from. 'Though I've never heard of red ones. Or maybe it's green, depending on how you look at it.'

'It's unheard of, finding something like this,' said Miss Brown, looking worried. 'We should tell the restaurant.'

'But surely it belongs to Millie,' said Sam. 'She's the one who found it.'

Word of Millie's discovery was spreading fast. Some of the pupils on the other tables left their places to get a closer look. Nate wanted to come over too, by the looks of it, but Mr. Ryan held him back. Out of the corner of her eye, Millie glimpsed the woman in the fur jacket gabbling ever more furiously into her phone.

One of the waiters trotted over to see what was afoot. When he saw what Millie had found, he lost his sang-froid and became quite emotional. 'C'est pas vrai! Je n'ai jamais vu une telle chose! C'est magnifique!'

'What's he saying?' whispered Paula.

'He's saying he's never seen anything like it,' said Millie. '*I've* never seen anything like it either. It really is a pearl, isn't it. A real one!'

The waiter said something to Miss Brown, who shook her head firmly. Mr. Ryan joined them and listened in before going into a huddle with Miss Brown. Millie heard her say, 'The parents will kill us. We'll lose our jobs,' to which Mr. Ryan replied, 'Three bottles between thirty? Plus there's us. It'll be a sip, at most. What harm can it do?'

He nodded at the waiter, who scurried off.

Mr. Ryan made the announcement to the class: 'Well, people, it seems the restaurant is treating us to champagne to celebrate Millie's discovery of a rare pearl in one of her oysters. As you know, alcohol is strictly forbidden on school trips. On this occasion, however, we're going to make an exception, since the quantities involved are so very, very small. But if I catch any of you abusing our trust and using this tiny mouthful as a pretext for delinquent behaviour, you're going to have to answer to me, and to Miss Cooper when we get back, and there *will* be hell to pay. Now, is anyone here taking any sort of prescription medicine?'

A couple of hands went up, but uncertainly, because their owners didn't want to miss out. Millie thought Mr. Ryan was taking a big risk, but she had never tasted champagne before, so she welcomed the chance to take even just a sip. Paris, oysters, pearls, champagne... What a day of firsts this was turning out to be.

While the waiter was setting out special flute-shaped glasses for the champagne, Millie sniffed her fingers and realised they smelt fishy. She got to her feet.

'Where are you off to, Millie?' asked Miss Brown.

'Just going to wash my hands.'

'It's through there,' said Miss Brown, pointing. 'Right at the back, then turn left.'

'Don't forget your pearl,' said Sam.

'Why?' said Millie. 'You think someone's going to steal it?'

'You never know,' said Sam. 'It's probably worth a bit.'

'OK, then,' said Millie, picking it up. 'I should probably rinse it anyway.'

'Get a move on,' said Paula, clapping her hands. 'You don't want to miss out on the bubbly.'

'Don't drop it down the plughole!' said Sam.

Millie grabbed her backpack, wove her way through the tables towards the back of the restaurant, and turned the corner into the ladies' cloakroom, where she washed her hands thoroughly. Then she rinsed the pearl under the tap, but carefully, remembering Sam's warning.

She'd been so taken aback by the discovery that she hadn't examined it properly until now. It was rather ugly, she decided. The red was the colour of dried blood, and even the green was not the life-giving green of grass or plants, but more like something old and mouldy. But it really *was* a pearl, and it was hers. *She* had found it, and now it struck her as rather more exotic and interesting than the perfectly shaped cultured pearls her mother always wore around her neck.

Millie was already wondering what to do with her find when she got home. She couldn't show it to her parents; they would surely want to know where she had got it. Still mulling over this conundrum, she wrapped her treasure in a paper tissue and stowed it in the zipped pocket of her backpack.

But as she emerged from the washroom, something even more unexpected happened. One of the waiters rushed up to her, saying, 'Miss! Miss!', and started babbling in a breathless whisper that was only half audible, though there was no one except Millie near enough to hear him.

'Miss! Miss! You are with the English party, yes?'

Millie recognised the waiter as the one she'd seen speaking to the woman in the silver dress, and nodded hesitantly.

The waiter grabbed her sleeve and tugged at it urgently. 'Your friend is in trouble. She needs your help! Quickly!'

'Which friend?' asked Millie, infected by the man's panic. 'Do you mean Paula? What happened?'

The waiter looked around wildly.

'Paula, yes! She asked for you. It's an emergency! We have no time to lose.'

Millie swallowed her alarm. She knew that if she was to be of any help at all, she needed to keep a clear head.

'What happened? Where is she?'

'This way. I take you.'

The waiter grasped her firmly by the elbow and steered her towards a door marked PRIVATE at the very back of the restaurant.

'In here.'

He opened the door, and bundled her through.

Millie looked around in confusion. She was in a windowless room lined with coat-hooks and lockers. There was no sign of Paula, or indeed of anyone else.

It didn't take long for her to realise that something was horribly wrong.

Chapter 6
Dead People

One part of Millie's brain registered a small metallic click, but it wasn't until later that she realised the significance of the sound.

A pair of trainers lay discarded on the floor. On the far wall was a sink with a dripping tap. The small room reeked of stale tobacco and dirty socks. And there was another smell beneath that - a strong but not unpleasant floral odour that seemed to be coming from somewhere behind her.

'Where is she?' Millie asked again, turning back towards the waiter just as he was lunging towards her, as if to give her a hug. More by instinct than design, she avoided him by stepping to one side. He instantly straightened up, looking guilty and embarrassed, and pretended to be examining a padlock on the door of the nearest locker.

Millie glimpsed something white bunched up in his hand - a handkerchief, she guessed. This, she realised now, was the source of the floral smell. 'Qu'est-ce...qu'est-ce que vous, er...' She realised her French wasn't up to it, and she was too flustered to think of the right words anyway, so fell back on basic English. 'What the hell do you think you're doing?'

The waiter grimaced, and instead of replying repositioned himself so that he was blocking her route back into the restaurant. Millie's heart was thudding, but she felt more angry than frightened. What did this creep want? Was he trying to steal the pearl? The smell of whatever the handkerchief had been soaked in was stronger now, and she began to feel a bit dizzy.

'Get out of my way!' She was thankful to hear her voice sounding a lot fiercer than she felt.

'You will come with me,' the waiter said, menacing her with the handkerchief again. 'It is better that way. Nobody will be hurt.'

'I'm not going anywhere with you,' Millie said, just as he lunged again. Once again she tried to sidestep, but this time her feet got tangled up in his. Feeling herself beginning to topple, she grabbed at a coat suspended from one of the hooks, and managed to keep her balance.

The waiter wasn't so lucky. He stumbled forward and the top of his head struck one of the lockers with a hollow crash. He righted himself shakily, bringing his hand up to his head as if intending to assess possible damage to his skull. But he'd forgotten about the handkerchief. Before he could stop himself, he'd inhaled the fumes. His eyes rolled back in his head, his knees buckled and he slumped sideways.

Millie watched all this as though seeing it through somebody else's eyes. She couldn't believe what was happening. Had the world gone mad? She had to get out of there, and fast, before this man recovered. She hurled herself at the door they'd come through, but now it wouldn't open. She panicked, pounding on it with her fist and tugging uselessly at the handle. Why wouldn't it open? Only then did she remember the metallic click she'd heard earlier and realise what it must have been: the sound of a key turning in the lock.

But the key wasn't in the lock now. She forced herself to calm down. The waiter probably still had it somewhere about his person. She really didn't want to touch him, but there wasn't much choice. She crouched down and began to fish around in his waistcoat pockets. He mumbled something under his breath and she froze, but he didn't seem to be coming round. Luckily she found the key quickly, which meant there was no need to explore his trouser pockets as well.

She returned to the door and, with trembling fingers, unlocked it and stepped back into the convivial hubbub of the restaurant, dragging the door shut behind her.

And found herself face to face with Nate McIntyre, his face cloudy with suspicion.

'What's going on?'

Millie sighed. Not again. She'd already had enough Nate for one day. 'Let me past, please.'

'Not before you tell me what's happening. Where've you been? What's in there?' Nate jerked his head at the closed door. He seemed determined not to let her pass until she gave him answers. So Millie lost her temper and kicked him hard, on the shin.

It must have hurt, because he breathed in sharply through his teeth. He didn't stand aside, but Millie pushed past with such force he couldn't stop her.

'You're the last person I'd tell,' she muttered before making her way back to her table, flushed and dishevelled.

'Millie! Where've you been?' asked Paula. 'I've saved some fizz for you.' She held out a glass flute with a minuscule amount of liquid in the bottom.

'We had to stop Paula from drinking it,' said Sam.

Miss Brown looked over at her anxiously. 'What's the matter, Millie? You haven't been sick again, have you?'

Millie grabbed her glass as she sat down and drained it in one gulp. 'One of the waiters tried to kidnap me.'

'What?' Miss Brown seemed more puzzled than alarmed.

'One of the waiters,' Millie repeated. 'He lured me into a locker room and tried to knock me out with something, I don't think it was chloroform. It smelt like perfume, only stronger. We should call the police.'

For a while, no one said anything. Millie was too busy collecting her thoughts to ask herself why they were all so silent, but then she looked round at their faces. Paula, Sam, Philip, Miss Brown, Bonetta, Chandra... They were all gazing at her. Paula and Sam seemed disappointed, Miss Brown and Philip more than a little concerned. Bonetta, on the other hand, was grinning from ear to ear. But they all had that expression you sometimes see on people visiting a doddery old relative, as if they'd had enough of her crazed babbling but didn't want to upset her.

Not one of them believed her story about the waiter, that much was obvious.

Millie looked over to the next table for help, hoping that Nate, at least, would back her up, then remembered that he hadn't seen anything. And even if he had, she thought, he was hardly going to take her side after she'd kicked him in the shin.

'It's true,' she said, looking at the sceptical expressions around her. 'Honestly. Why on earth would I make up a story like that?'

'Maybe because you're a drama queen?' suggested Bonetta. 'Like that so-called fit you threw on the train? Please! Anyone could see you were faking.'

'I was not!' Millie said, feeling her ears go red.

'Cut it out, Bonetta,' said Paula, who reached out and took one of Millie's hands in her own, and then started stroking it, like a compassionate nurse tending to a hysterical patient. And that was it, thought Millie. They all thought she was a fantasist, making up wild stories to get attention.

'So you're not going to call the police?' she asked Miss Brown, who was now just looking embarrassed.

'And that stupid pearl!' Bonetta continued, bitterness etched into her voice.

For the first time, it occurred to Millie that Bonetta was madly jealous of her, though she couldn't for the life of her imagine why.

'I bet you had it with you all along,' said Bonetta. 'You just *pretended* to find it in the oyster.'

'Don't be ridiculous,' said Millie. 'Why would I do something like that?'

'That's enough, Bonetta,' said Miss Brown, more embarrassed than ever. 'Are you sure you're all right, Millie? Maybe you shouldn't have had those oysters.'

'Oh, I'm fine,' Millie said, a bit sarcastically, because she wasn't feeling fine at all. That waiter had tried to kidnap her! What if he tried to kidnap someone else? What if he was going around, kidnapping teenage girls and selling them to slave traders?

But she couldn't see why anyone might want to kidnap her instead of one of the prettier or wealthier girls in the class. Marcus and Aurelia Greenwood were neither rich nor famous; they weren't the sort of people who would be able to pay an enormous ransom. What had the waiter wanted from her, then? The pearl? It had to be something to do with the pearl! But if that was so, why hadn't he just asked her for it?

All Millie's classmates, except for the ones who were on diets, were now ordering dessert, but Millie had lost her appetite. She sensed that her friends were just humouring her, trying to draw her into inconsequential chit-chat about TV or celebrities, or swapping spoonfuls of chocolate gâteau and comparing it, very favourably, to the faded pastries on offer at the Five-Star.

Millie felt awkward and humiliated. No one mentioned the pearl again, and she realised it was a waste of time trying to make them believe her story about the attempted kidnapping. In fact, she found she didn't feel like talking much anyway. It wasn't even as though she *liked* being the centre of attention; she couldn't help it if strange things were happening to her. She just wanted to fade into the wallpaper and be invisible again.

She could feel her features collapsing into one of her famous scowls, but she no longer cared. The uglier, the better, she decided. Maybe people would stop bugging her then.

She spotted the waiter from the locker room on the other side of the restaurant, serving plates of food as though nothing had happened. He looked a little unsteady on his feet, but no matter how hard she stared at him, willing him to turn and look her in the eye, he obstinately refused to meet her gaze.

Once again, she felt angry. It wasn't fair! It would serve everybody right if she really *had* been kidnapped. Maybe they would have been sorry then.

She sat fuming in silence until it was time to go, when she got up and put on her jacket. It was while she was winding the red scarf around her neck that she noticed the woman in the silver dress glaring at her ferociously. Millie was by now in such a foul mood that she forgot her manners and glared straight back.

For a moment, the woman looked taken aback at the English girl's effrontery. But then she said something to her dining companion and smiled. It was a ghastly smile that showed far too many teeth, and for an instant it made her face look like a grinning skull. The sight made Millie's skin crawl. Maybe it wasn't good to be that skinny after all. She pointedly turned her back on the couple and joined the others filing out of the brasserie, only vaguely aware that the woman had stood up and was following them outside.

The pupils spilled out into the street, laughing and chattering. Millie was going along with them silently, and a little sullenly, when she felt someone tug at her sleeve. She turned, half-expecting to see the grinning skull again, but the woman now facing her couldn't have been more of a contrast to the skinny socialite in the silver dress. This woman was short and plumpish, wrapped in a voluminous maroon velvet cloak, a green felt hat perched jauntily on her head, wild strands of curly red hair escaping from beneath it like unruly capillaries.

She looked too well dressed to be homeless, but her clothes marked her out as eccentric, and perched on her shoulder was a magpie. The bird tilted its head so it could fix Millie with one of its beady eyes.

'I'm sorry,' said Millie. 'I don't have any spare change.'

'Camille! Ma petite Camille!' The plump woman gabbled something else in rapid French, and tried to enfold Millie in her arms.

The magpie let out a small 'Caw!'

'I'm sorry,' Millie said again, trying to tear herself away and feeling a great weariness descend on her. Was this another stupid kidnap attempt? Did she have a notice pinned to her back inviting complete strangers to come up to her and try their luck? 'You must be mistaking me for someone else,' she said, but the woman clung on, and kept babbling.

And then someone else had stepped between them and was pushing the woman away and growling, 'Get out of here! Leave her alone!'

It was Nate. Millie didn't know whether to feel grateful or annoyed, but before she even had a chance to decide whether or not to thank him, Miss Brown was ushering her on to the bus and the pressure of people lining up behind her was carrying her down the aisle.

She turned to look for Nate, but he had already slipped into a seat at the front, where he was glowering at the doors as though he expected a gang of bus hijackers to burst in through them at any second.

Paula was in the seat next to Sam, and the place next to Philip was already occupied by Chandra, so Millie ended up sitting on her own and feeling sorry for herself again. As the engine started up, she looked out of the window and saw the woman in the velvet coat had somehow wedged herself in the doorway of the brasserie, so that no one was able to get in or out. The magpie had risen a few inches into the air and was flapping its wings in someone's face. There was an untidy pile-up of people just inside the door, where there appeared to be some sort of tussle going on.

As the bus began to move, the woman in the velvet coat gazed anxiously up at Millie, and nodded. There was something so solicitous in her expression that, for a moment, Millie was reminded of how her parents had looked at her from the bus stop, the last time she'd seen them.

And then the bus was moving away.

*****

The sun, reluctant to show itself all day, had finally given up the ghost and was now sulking behind a vast bank of threatening cloud.

The pupils left the bus and lined up in front of the gates of the cemetery while Mr. Ryan counted heads. The breeze had picked up force, and was whipping dead leaves and pieces of discarded paper along the pavements.

Philip scanned the sky anxiously, and said, 'I hope it's not going to rain.'

'I'm freezing,' said Paula, who did indeed look underdressed in her pink jacket. She tugged her collar up around her neck, and hunched her shoulders, stamping her feet.

Millie was still smarting from the unjust way she'd been treated in the restaurant, but her friend's violent shivering brought her back to her senses. 'Here,' she said, unwinding her red scarf. 'You can borrow this, if you like.'

Paula stepped back with an almost comical look of outrage on her face, as though Millie had just offered her a boa constrictor. 'I can't wear that!'

'It's OK,' said Millie. 'My jacket's warmer than yours, and if I get really cold I can put my hood up.'

'No,' said Paula. 'I mean, I can't *possibly* wear red! It clashes with my jacket!'

Millie couldn't tell if Paula was joking, but just then there was an extra-strong gust of wind. Paula shrieked and snatched the scarf out of Millie's grasp and began to wind it around her neck.

The others were already following Mrs. Fletcher through the imposing limestone gateway into the cemetery.

'Paula! Millie!' barked Mr. Ryan. 'Come along now! No dilly-dallying!'

'It's all right for him,' grumbled Paula as they caught up. 'He couldn't care less about fashion.'

'You're right about that,' giggled Millie. 'Look at him, he's all done up like an Eskimo.' She was beginning to feel better, and had already forgiven Paula for sitting next to Sam on the bus, and for not believing her story about the waiter. Now that she thought about it, it had seemed pretty far-fetched.

But it *had* happened!

They took the main avenue into the cemetery. Thanks to the grey skies and cold wind, there was only a sparse smattering of other visitors.

'It's a city of the dead,' Millie observed as they passed between the tightly packed ranks of tombs and marble monuments. She glanced down a side avenue and spied a flock of crows as big as cats, hopping and pecking at the tufts of grass sprouting between the graves. They made her think of the magpie on the eccentric woman's shoulder, but that had seemed almost cute compared to these monsters.

'Mutant crows,' said Paula. ''That's all we need.'

''They'll peck your eyeballs out if you're not careful,' said Philip.

They plunged further into the cemetery, forced into single file as Mrs. Fletcher led the way off the main drag, up some narrow steps and stopped in front of a monument adorned with marble carvings.

'Gather round,' she ordered as her pupils formed an untidy half-circle, most of them pulling their collars up or winding their scarves more tightly as they tried to shield themselves from the brisk wind. 'Anyone recognise this?'

There was a low murmur before Cressida Hartley piped up. 'It's like that painting we saw in the Louvre. The one with all those people on the raft.'

'Correct!' said Mrs. Fletcher, looking as though she were having the time of her life. 'It's a bas-relief of that painting we saw, The Raft of the Medusa. And this is the tomb of the man who painted it: Théodore Géricault, one of the pioneers of the French Romantic movement, who died at the age of forty-three after falling off his horse.'

She and Mr. Ryan began to hand out sheets of paper. Millie took one and looked at it. It was a map of the cemetery. Some of the graves were marked with numbered red dots, each dot representing one of Père Lachaise's illustrious dead residents. Millie skimmed the list and found to her surprise that she recognised only a few of the names.

'Now, people, your class project is to select one of the graves marked in red, and then, when you get back to school, find out all you can about the person who's buried there, and write an essay about their lives, and why we still remember them. In French, please!'

There was a mildly rebellious murmur. Russell Jones said what all of them were thinking. 'But we *don't* remember them! I've never heard of any of these people!'

'That's right,' said Mrs. Fletcher, her face lighting up as she warmed to her subject. 'You may never have heard of them, but that's what you're here for - to learn! I don't suppose any of you have heard of Gérard de Nerval, for example, but he was an interesting character: a poet who had a pet lobster he took for walks at the end of a blue ribbon. He drank wine out of a goblet made from his father's skull, and ended up hanging himself with the Queen of Sheba's garter.'

'He was quite mad,' Mr. Ryan chipped in, lest anyone had thought these the actions of a perfectly sane person.

'A lot of these people led very colourful lives,' said Mrs. Fletcher. 'I don't think you'll find them boring. There are artists, and writers, and musicians, and actors, and singers. You've all heard of Edith Piaf, haven't you? *Je ne regrette rien...*' She rolled her Rs exaggeratedly. 'Spread out, and try not to choose the same grave as everyone else - there are more than enough to go round. Mr. Ryan, Miss Brown and I will be around if you have questions. Meet back at the main gate at four thirty, prompt. Now - off you go!'

She clapped her hands twice. Grateful to be left to their own devices, the pupils melted away in twos and threes until only Millie, Paula, Philip and Sam were left behind.

Millie followed Mrs. Fletcher, who had slipped behind one of the monuments and was in the process of extracting a packet of cigarettes from her coat pocket. When she saw Millie, she hurriedly pushed the packet back out of sight and stood there looking awkward. 'You mustn't smoke, Millie,' she said unnecessarily. 'It's bad for your health.'

'Excuse me, Mrs. Fletcher,' said Millie, 'but Oscar Wilde's grave isn't marked on the paper.'

'That's because he's English,' said Mrs. Fletcher.

'Irish, actually,' said Millie.

Mrs. Fletcher didn't appear to have heard. 'I'm impressed you know about Wilde, but do bear in mind that today is really an extended French lesson. So I want you to pick the grave of someone who was French.'

Millie rejoined the others, a little disappointed.

'Well Millie, who's it to be?' asked Philip.

'I don't know,' said Millie. 'Maybe Proust...'

'Who he?' asked Sam.

It didn't surprise Millie in the slightest that Sam hadn't heard of one of the most famous French writers of all time.

'He wrote a very long novel that hardly anyone has read, though I expect I'll get round to reading it one day,' she explained. 'He wrote in a room lined with cork, so he wouldn't be disturbed by outside noise.'

'Whoopee,' Paula said without much enthusiasm. She blew on her hands, which were now turning a delicate shade of blue. She hadn't even thought to bring gloves. 'So what shall we do? Come on, I'm freezing.'

Philip was going through the list and suddenly came across a name that made him perk up. 'Georges Méliès! You know he was one of the first film directors? Practically invented special effects! I'm off to find him. Who's with me?'

He paused, obviously waiting for Paula to reply, but she didn't. Philip struggled not to look hurt, then turned his back on them and hurried off, map in hand.

'Well,' said Paula, whose attempts to keep warm by stamping her feet were stymied by her absurdly flimsy shoes.

'Let's go and see Jim Morrison,' suggested Sam.

'He's not on the list,' said Millie. 'Also, he's American.'

'Who cares,' said Sam. 'Come on, let's take a look. It's too cold to stand around doing nothing.'

He set off at a brisk pace. Paula dawdled for a few seconds before coming to a decision and scampering after him. After a few steps she turned and asked Millie, 'You coming?'

Millie hesitated, not wanting to waste her time on a grave that wasn't on the list. Besides, Paula's invitation had sounded distinctly half-hearted.

'I think I'll look for Balzac,' Millie called after her. 'I'll come and meet you at Jim Morrison afterwards.'

'Right you are, Mill,' said Paula, who had picked up Sam's habit of truncating her name. 'See you later.' She gave Millie an absent-minded wave before turning back to catch up with Sam.

Millie watched the red scarf disappear behind the trees as Paula and Sam turned off the path and started weaving their way between the tombs. Then she consulted the map in search of Honoré de Balzac. She'd read two of his novels and enjoyed them, even though the characters had been horrible people.

Balzac's tomb, topped by a bronze bust of the writer, wasn't far away, but as she approached, she saw a gaggle of classmates already clustered around it. Brian Erskine was there, and Simon, and Dyson and Katy and a couple of others.

Probably because the tomb was easy to find, Millie thought. She found it hard to believe any of them were actually *interested* in Balzac or his books. They probably hadn't even heard of him, let alone read anything he'd written. Ah well, she would just have to choose somebody else. But who? She doubled back the way she'd come and, on an impulse she would soon come to regret, climbed a narrow flight of stone steps leading to a twisty path, where there was no one else in sight.

The problem was, now she was alone, she wasn't sure she liked it. This was a cemetery, after all, and a bit spooky, and she couldn't shake off the feeling she was being watched.

The wind rustled in the trees. Overhead, ominous dark clouds were scudding across the grey sky. A giant crow watched her from the roof of a small mausoleum and let out a loud croak that made her jump. The further away she got from Balzac, the more she wished she'd stuck with him after all. At least that way she would now be surrounded by live people as well as dead ones.

She stared at the map and tried to work out exactly where she was, but away from the major avenues it was hard to distinguish one path from another. Apparently there was a crematorium up ahead, but she couldn't see it for the trees. Maybe she would just head straight down to meet Paula and Sam at Jim Morrison. She noticed Morrison's tomb wasn't far from a monument to Abelard and Héloïse; she knew they were tragic lovers who had lived and died in medieval times, but that was about it. Perhaps it would be fun to find out more about them.

She thrust her hands deep into her pockets and began to walk in what she hoped was the right direction, trying not to feel intimidated by the big black crows that now seemed to be lining her path, perched on the roofs of family graves, on monuments and crosses, gazing down at her as she passed. No wonder she felt as though she were being watched. They were just birds, she told herself, though unusually bold ones. She paused and tried to outstare the nearest crow, but it simply stared back without flinching, its head turned to one side so it could fix her with its beady eye, like the magpie outside the brasserie.

The crow suddenly flapped its wings, rose a few feet into the air and came to rest on a black marble tombstone a few feet ahead of her. A bunch of lilies lay on the grave. The flowers looked almost fresh, Millie thought as she edged closer, trying to read the words etched in the marble.

NICOLAS ET ÉVANGÉLINE VERTBOIS
QUE LA MORT LES RÉUNISSE EN PAIX

Vertbois, thought Millie. *Vertbois*. How odd. *Vert* was the French word for green, and *bois* was wood. *Greenwood.* She chuckled softly at the coincidence. Perhaps, if she had been born in France, she would have been Millie Vertbois, instead of Millie Greenwood.

For once, she wished she had a smartphone so she could have taken a picture of the grave, but she hadn't, so there was nothing to do but press on. Maybe one day she would come back with a camera.

There was another gust of wind, so vicious it made her shiver. The breeze made the leaves rustle like tissue paper.

The odd thing was, the leaves carried on rustling even after the breeze had stopped blowing.

The rustling seemed especially loud behind her. She looked round, and glimpsed someone moving through the trees.

At first, Millie though it was Sissy Urquhart, who sometimes had a tendency to drift around like that, as though not quite sure of where she was, or what she was supposed to be doing. But then Millie realised that not even Sissy moved in that peculiar flitting way, darting from tomb to tomb and then ducking out of sight, so that Millie couldn't get a really good look at her.

And after a moment, she realised she didn't *want* to get a good look at that figure. In fact, she wanted to move as far away as possible from it, and fast.

She turned her back on it and began to stride faster and faster along the path. When she reckoned she'd put a safe distance between her and the figure she now knew wasn't Sissy, she took a look over her shoulder.

It was closer than ever.

And the rustling was louder now. The figure was wispy, and pale grey, Millie saw now, the colour of ashes, and wearing what appeared to be a long grey scarf that fluttered behind it, through the tombs, though when Millie tried to focus on it she found she wasn't sure that it *was* a scarf. It could have been smoke. The figure's movements were strange and rhythmic; it was swaying from side to side, torso and arms undulating in a serpentine way so that it was hard to tell where the figure stopped and the dress began. Almost as though it were dancing, as if to some sort of music inaudible to Millie's ears. Maybe it was dancing to the rustling sound. Or maybe the figure itself was the source of the rustling.

The more Millie thought about it, the more that seemed likely.

The worst of it was that, now she really looked at it, the figure's head seemed bent at an angle to the neck that didn't seem natural. Nobody's necks, not even dancers' necks, were supposed to bend at ninety degrees like that. And the head was spoiling the illusion of gracefulness by flopping heavily around as the figure moved. The movements of the head were not rhythmic at all, not even a little bit.

And the figure continued to dance and flutter, coming closer.

Chapter 7
Jim Morrison's Tomb

Millie decided that she definitely did *not* want the fluttering figure to catch up with her. She didn't want to see it any more clearly than she could see it now, which was already bad enough. So she turned her back on it again and began to walk as fast as she could. She wanted to run, but sensed this would be a bad idea because the paving stones were uneven and the last thing she needed was to stumble and fall. If she fell, that thing would easily be able to catch up with her, and then it would bend over her, and then put its face right up against hers... And then... And then...

It didn't bear thinking about.

The path twisted and turned. Where was everyone? Surely there must be someone else in this part of the cemetery. Millie's breath was coming out of her in sharp little gasps. There was a stitch stabbing into her side. She felt as though she were the only living person in this city of the dead. It was an uncomfortable thought, one she tried to push to the back of her head, because she knew that if she were the only living person here, that would mean the figure behind her...

The last thing she wanted to admit, even to herself, was that the person behind her, flitting through the graves, its head wobbling at ninety degrees to its neck, was not a living thing at all.

Millie looked over her shoulder again, and was barely able to suppress the shriek of horror that rose to her lips. The figure was even closer, darting in and out among the tombs and the trees like a will-o'-the-wisp. She felt cold to her bones, and this time it wasn't the wind that was making her shiver.

The path twisted again. Now the risk of falling over was the least of Millie's concerns. She didn't care any more; she had to get away from that dancing figure, no matter what. So she broke into a run, taking the bend at full tilt.

And ran slap bang into Ayesha Washington, nearly knocking her over.

'Hey, watch it!' said Ayesha.

Walking alongside her were Simon Ashworth and Kevin Marshall. Millie had never been so happy to see them, even though she didn't like Kevin much.

'Hey, what's the rush?' he said.

Millie bent forward and put her hands on her knees and tried to catch her breath. 'I thought... I just thought...' She glanced back. The wispy grey figure was gone.

'Graveyard spooked you?' said Simon. 'Whooooh, watch out! Millie's seen a ghost!'

Millie laughed weakly. She had an awful feeling that Simon was right.

'I was just looking for Paula,' she said, feeling a bit foolish. 'And Sam.'

'We passed them back there,' said Ayesha, pointing down the path.

Millie sensed the three of them were waiting for her to say or do something. They didn't seem particularly thrilled to see her, but that wasn't unusual; they were never mean to her, like Nate or Bonetta, but nor did they seek out her company. They lived parallel lives that only rarely intersected. And now Ayesha was looking impatient, as though Millie had interrupted important business that couldn't be resumed until she'd moved on.

Millie hovered, not wanting to find herself alone again. But then there was a shout of 'Millie!' behind her. She turned and saw Nate coming up fast. Even from this distance she could feel the waves of fury coming off him. The sight spurred her into action.

'See you later!' she gasped, and left Ayesha and the two boys gaping after her as she sprinted away.

Fortunately, she had a head start on Nate. She darted left, and then turned right, and then went down another narrow flight of crumbling steps, until she was pretty sure she'd thrown him off her tail. And mercifully, in this part of the cemetery she was no longer alone. She passed several clusters of tourists, and old people carrying flowers. Millie wondered if they had relatives buried nearby; as far as she knew, people were still being buried here. She consulted her map again. Jim Morrison's grave was in Section Six, around the corner.

She turned into the next avenue and glimpsed a sudden riot of colour up ahead, spilling out from behind a small mausoleum. Morrison's grave was festooned with offerings of posies and potted plants, and she spotted a flash of red there as well. It had to be Paula in the scarf!

Millie started forward...

And stopped dead, unable to believe her eyes.

Neither Paula nor Sam saw her. Sam had his back to her. Paula was facing Millie, but she was too busy kissing Sam to notice anyone but him.

After the first shock, Millie felt like running right up to them and snatching her scarf from Paula's neck, or - even better - throttling her with it, but that would have meant announcing her presence, and she didn't want either of them knowing she was there. She didn't understand why, but she felt embarrassed, and ashamed.

So she stood and stared for a few moments, feeling a stab of anguish in her chest, worse than any stitch, and thinking, so that's what it feels like to have a broken heart, before the dread of them catching sight of her trumped the inertia, and she turned her back on the awful scene and walked away as fast as she could.

She could feel herself blushing scarlet with humiliation. What an idiot she'd been, thinking Sam was interested in her. How could she have been so stupid? Hot tears were pricking at her eyes, but she blinked them away furiously. No, she would *not* cry. So much for Paula's rule about not trespassing on friends' territory. Well, that was clearly a load of rot. Paula just did whatever she wanted, and everyone else could go hang. She'd *known* Millie liked Sam. And obviously didn't give a fig.

Millie barely noticed as she twisted her ankle on a broken paving stone and stumbled against an unkempt bush, where a sharp twig slapped her across the face, but that was nothing compared to the whiplash of emotions tossing her around. Only a few moments ago, she'd been terrified out of her wits. And here she was now, seething with anger at having been betrayed by her best friend. She didn't know where she was going any more, and she didn't care. It was obvious now that Sam had only ever been nice to her in order to get closer to Paula. Well, the two of them deserved each other, and Millie was never going to speak to either of them ever again.

She passed an elaborate sculpture of an angel slumped over a corpse, thought it looked familiar, and realised she'd been stomping around in angry circles. Still blinking back tears, she studied the map again, trying to see through the mist and concentrate on the topography. Barely aware of what she was doing, she sought out the memorial to Abelard and Héloïse, found it, stared at it for five minutes without really seeing it, then went on to the tomb of the writer Colette, whose books she hadn't read but which were on her to-do list.

From Colette's tomb, she was able to see the front gate. She checked her watch. Still ten minutes before the class was due to meet up, but no point in going any deeper into the cemetery now. She didn't want to risk running into Paula and Sam, and she *definitely* didn't want to see that wispy figure in grey again.

The memory of it made her laugh bitterly to herself. At the time, she'd thought that grey figure was the absolute worst thing she could have seen, but now it seemed like small beer next to the dreadful spectacle that had greeted her at Jim Morrison's tomb.

She walked, very slowly, to the front gate, where Mr. Ryan was deep in conversation with Miss Brown. When they noticed her approaching they immediately stopped talking and stood up straight, ensuring there was a respectable distance between them.

'Hello Millie,' said Mr. Ryan. 'Did you find any interesting graves?'

'One or two,' Millie replied in a monotone.

'Feeling OK?' Miss Brown asked. 'No more problems with, er, waiters?'

'I'm fine!' Millie snapped, so sharply that the two teachers exchanged looks.

'Well, that's good,' said Miss Brown. 'I think it was very intrepid of you to try those oysters.'

Millie wished Miss Brown hadn't mentioned oysters, because now she thought about it, she really did feel slightly sick. She didn't think it had anything to do with anything she'd had for lunch, though.

Her classmates started turning up in dribs and drabs. Nate passed uncomfortably close, and scowled at her so unpleasantly that she looked down at her shoes, thinking he was the least of her problems now. She wondered what to say to Paula and Sam when they turned up. Maybe it was best to keep quiet, pretend she hadn't seen anything. She wished she could turn back time and decide not to go to Jim Morrison's tomb after all. But what good would that have done? Even if she hadn't seen it, it would still have happened.

Someone touched her elbow. She looked up and saw Philip.

'Where's Paula?' he asked.

'With Sam,' said Millie.

There was something in her tone that made Philip peer at her curiously, but she didn't trust herself to say anything more. She wondered if Philip would be as upset as she was when he found out. *If* he found out. Maybe Paula and Sam weren't going to admit anything. They hadn't seen Millie. As far as they were aware, no one knew they'd been snogging.

Mrs. Fletcher finished counting heads. 'That's twenty-eight. Who's missing?'

Mr. Ryan craned his neck. 'Sam? Sam Tulliver? Anyone seen him?'

'And Paula,' Philip spoke up. 'She's not here either.'

Mr. Ryan sighed. 'Sam Tulliver and Paula O'Keefe. Anyone seen either of them?'

'We saw them earlier,' said Simon Ashworth.

'Millie was looking for them, said Ayesha.

All eyes turned towards Millie. She swallowed, feeling everyone staring at her. 'I saw them at Jim Morrison's tomb,' she said at last. 'Maybe twenty minutes ago.'

'What were they doing there?' asked Mr. Ryan, visibly annoyed. 'Jim Morrison wasn't on the list.'

Millie felt a small flurry of spiteful satisfaction, hoping she'd managed to get Paula and Sam a ticking-off, at the very least.

'Maybe they're still there,' said Miss Brown. 'Do they have phones?'

'Paula's got hers,' said Katy Wilson. 'She texted me on the train.'

'What's her number?' Miss Brown got her own phone out and tapped in Paula's number as Katy read it off her own phone. Miss Brown listened for a few moments, frowning, then said, 'Paula, get a move on. We're all waiting for you at the gate.'

She looked up. 'Straight to message.'

Mr. Ryan was tapping his foot impatiently. 'Where's Jim Morrison anyway?'

Mrs. Fletcher showed him on the map, and he took off at a canter.

'OK,' said Mrs. Fletcher. 'The rest of you might as well get on the bus.'

As they filed out of the gates, Nate drew level with Millie and hissed, 'This is all your fault! Why did you have to be so stupid? This wouldn't have happened if you'd...'

But the rest of his sentence was lost as Philip planted himself firmly between Nate and Millie. Mrs. Fletcher grabbed Nate's arm and hauled him backwards with a stern, 'Nate McIntyre! What were we talking about earlier?'

The pupils climbed back on to the bus, while Mrs. Fletcher and Miss Brown waited outside, Miss Brown checking her watch so often it began to look like a nervous tic. Millie installed herself in a seat near the back, as far away from Nate as possible; Philip sat next to her, putting his bag on the two seats across the aisle from them. No one had to ask who he was saving the places for.

Millie was still furious, but, as the minutes ticked away, her fury began to ebb, and was replaced by gnawing anxiety. Where had Paula got to? It wasn't as though she'd wanted to hang out in the cemetery any longer than was necessary; she wasn't even dressed properly for this cold weather. Were she and Sam still kissing somewhere? How could they have lost track of time? Millie felt the anger welling up inside her again.

Philip said something, but she wasn't listening. She stared out of the window at the cemetery gate, willing Paula and Sam to appear, but instead saw Mr. Ryan trotting back on his own. He went into a huddle with Miss Brown and Mrs. Fletcher, who eventually climbed on to the bus without him and told the driver to close the door. The teachers were looking tight-lipped and not at all happy. Outside, Mr. Ryan turned away from the bus with a harried wave and scurried back towards the lodge by the gate.

'OK, people,' said Miss Brown. 'We're off now. We have a train to catch.' She bent over to say something to the driver. The engine started and the bus slowly started to turn round.

'No!' cried Millie, standing up. 'We can't leave without them!'

'Sit down, Millie,' said Miss Brown. 'There's nothing to worry about. Mr. Ryan has gone to get them, and they'll catch up with us later.'

'But we can't leave them here,' Millie said to Philip. He got to his feet and went to the front, hanging on to the seatbacks as he went to keep his balance, and Millie watched as he started arguing with Mrs. Fletcher. She couldn't hear what they were saying, but eventually he gave up and came back and sat down beside her.

'Ryan couldn't find them,' he said. Unnecessarily, Millie thought, since that much had been obvious. 'Did they say anything when you saw them, Millie?'

Millie looked at him, longing to share her pain. 'I said I'd seen them,' she said carefully. 'I didn't say *they'd* seen *me*.'

Tears prickled at her eyes, but now she couldn't tell whether they were tears of anger or of feeling sorry for herself. Once again she felt like throttling Paula. Had she and Sam headed deeper into the cemetery so they could carry on snogging? Surely they knew there was a train to catch? How could they mess everyone around like this? Could they have *been* any more selfish? What if everyone missed the train, and Millie's parents found out where she had been and, worse, that Millie had forged her mother's signature?

And to think she'd been dumb enough to lend Paula her favourite scarf.

As the bus started off down the road she took one last look back at the cemetery gates, hoping against hope that she would see Sam and Paula running out, waving and laughing and trying to catch up. But there was no one there, not even Mr. Ryan now.

The atmosphere on the bus was subdued. Two of the most popular pupils were missing, and their absence left a disconcerting gap. Millie sensed everyone was whispering about Paula and Sam. Maybe she was the only one who hadn't known they fancied each other. Maybe they'd already been seen kissing at a party, or after school at the Five-Star, and she, Millie, was the last to know. That would be just typical, she thought bitterly. Life was passing her by, as always.

Philip wasn't saying much either. As the bus manoeuvred its way slowly through the late afternoon traffic, Millie cast a sideways glance at him and was taken aback to see the muscles in his jaw were clenched, as though he were struggling to hold his feelings in. If Paula and Sam were an item, it seemed Philip hadn't known about it any more than Millie had.

Millie wondered again whether to tell him, but decided not to. It wouldn't do any good now, not if Paula and Sam had done something idiotic, like eloping together. But Millie couldn't imagine either of them doing anything *that* silly and irresponsible. Paula might have joked about it, but she wouldn't have wanted to get into trouble, and Sam just wasn't the sort to do anything that stupid. Besides, from what Millie had overheard, he had football practice in the morning, and there was no way he would risk missing that.

There was another niggling thought at the back of her brain - a fanciful one, but even more worrying.

Reluctantly she considered it. What if... what if the waiter from the brasserie had followed them to the cemetery, and had kidnapped Paula and Sam?

No, she thought, shaking her head. No. That was absurd. Even if he'd tried to grab Paula the way he'd tried to grab Millie, Sam would have been there. Sam would have fought him off. Sam was taller than the waiter, and strong. The waiter would have been no match for him.

Unless he'd had help...

'What are you thinking?' Philip asked suddenly.

Millie shook her head to try and get rid of the dark thoughts that kept trying to crowd in on her. 'I was just... When we were in the restaurant...' She didn't know how to continue. 'Paula and I, we don't look anything like each other, do we? You wouldn't ever get us confused?'

Philip looked bewildered. 'Only if you were blind!' Then he seemed to think twice about what he'd said, as if Millie might interpret it as an insult. 'I mean, you've got different coloured hair. Maybe if one of you wore a wig or something.'

'Or maybe if we wore the same clothes,' Millie said to herself. 'Maybe if Paula wore my red scarf...'

Philip was looking at her curiously. 'What are you thinking?'

'Nothing,' Millie said quickly. 'I just wish I hadn't given Paula my scarf.'

'Oh well, I know how to remedy that.' Philip took off his own scarf and draped it around her neck. The wool was grey and coarse and a bit scratchy, but it was a sweet gesture and Millie felt touched.

'Crazy day, huh?' he said, trying to smile.

'It's been very strange...' She suddenly felt grateful Philip was there, and a bit selfish for not realising that he would be just as worried about Paula and Sam as she was. She tried to change the subject. 'Did you ever find that film director's grave? The special effects guy you were looking for?'

'Méliès? Yes...' But Philip wasn't about to be distracted. 'Where do you think they are? It's not like Sam to go AWOL like this.'

Millie shrugged helplessly. She wondered whether to tell Philip about the wispy grey figure she'd glimpsed flitting through the trees, but decided she didn't want him thinking she was imagining things again. The business with the waiter had been bad enough.

She unzipped the pocket of her backpack and slid her hand inside to check the pearl was still there, nestling misshapenly in its tissue. She had no idea what she would do with it when she got back to Bramblewood. Maybe she could sell it. But now she thought about that, she realised she didn't want to. The pearl was hers and no one else's. It had literally been presented to her on a plate. Almost as if *it* had chosen *her*.

But Bramblewood was still three hundred miles away, and Millie started to worry about the slowness of their progress towards the station. At the rate they were going, it began to look as though they might miss their train. The bus hadn't picked up much speed as it crawled along the busy Avenue de la République, but now, on the Boulevard de Magenta, it slowed down even more, and finally ground to a complete halt amid a cacophony of horns and angrily gesticulating drivers.

Millie peered out of the window at the gridlocked traffic, willing it to start moving again. But for fifteen minutes, they stayed where they were, without moving an inch. Miss Brown was checking her watch ever more frequently, and Mrs. Fletcher was pacing back and forth in the tiny space next to the driver.

'Isn't that the station up ahead?' asked Chandra. 'Can't we just get out and walk?'

'No, that's the Gare de l'Est,' said Miss Brown. 'The Eurostar goes from a different station, the Gare du Nord.'

Mrs. Fletcher had a word with the driver, and the doors opened and she got off. Millie saw her weaving through the unmoving vehicles and talking to a couple of gendarmes at the side of the road up ahead. They were shrugging and shaking their heads.

'What's happening?' someone asked loudly.

Stuart Barker slid open a window and stuck his head out further than was probably wise. 'I can see a bunch of people waving signs. They don't seem to be going anywhere, just blocking the road... No hang on... Hey, I can see a rhinoceros!'

The people around him sniggered and rolled their eyes. Stu would do anything for a cheap laugh, but this was more stupid than funny. But then Tim Chivers, who had also been peering out of the window, turned back and said, 'It *is!* It's a rhino!'

There was a mad scramble as the pupils rushed to the windows on the left of the bus, trying to see what was going on and completely ignoring Miss Brown's pleas for them to sit back down again. Millie couldn't see any elephants, but she saw some of the people with signs, who were spilling out between the cars and picking their way down the street. It appeared to be some sort of demonstration, but the protestors looked unusually well turned out, she thought, not at all like demonstrators she'd seen on the news. These men were dressed in formal suits, the women in party dresses or ballgowns. They were waving red and blue banners; the printing on them was illegible from this distance, but Millie could just about make out the words, 'NOUS SOMMES TOUS...' and 'À BAS LA...' and thought she could hear them chanting as they came, but that might have been her imagination because it was hard to hear anything over the racket of car horns.

As one of the women came nearer Millie saw her fur stole rippling, and in that instant realised to her horror that it wasn't a fur stole at all - it was a large black snake wound around the woman's bare shoulders, its head moving lazily. Millie uttered a little cry and grabbed Philip's forearm, but the woman had already stepped out of sight behind a van.

'Did you see that?'

But Philip was staring open-mouthed at something else. Millie followed his gaze to where a pair of zebras were eating the remains of a straw hat off the bonnet of a car, oblivious to the driver honking on his horn and yelling at them.

'Oh my God,' said Alison Moseby. 'Is that a wolf?'

'Who let the dogs out?' shrieked Russell Jones. ''The animals have escaped! Watch out for the tigers!'

'We're never going to get that train, are we?' Millie said in a small voice.

'It's OK, Millie,' said Philip. ''There's still loads of time.' But he didn't sound so sure.

'Oh no!' shouted Katy in mock panic. 'Looks like we're going to miss our train and have to spend the night in Paris! How awful!' There was laughter; Millie thought some of sounded a bit hysterical.

'No one's missing any train,' Miss Brown said, but, like Philip, she didn't sound very confident.

The door opened to let Mrs. Fletcher climb back on board. Now she too was gesticulating like the gendarmes.

Millie's heart sank even further as Nate got to his feet and made his way to the front of the bus, where he started speaking intently to the teachers. Millie couldn't hear him over the babble in the bus, but whatever he was saying was holding their attention.

After conferring with Miss Brown for a few moments, Mrs. Fletcher turned and clapped her hands loudly. 'Listen up, people!' She had to shout out several times before she had everyone's attention. 'We're going to get off this bus and walk to the station. It's only a few minutes from here, and Nate knows a shortcut. So grab your bags and get cracking. No shilly-shallying, please - we've got a train to catch, unless you want to pay double for the next one! Follow Nate!'

With one last glare at Millie, Nate got off the bus with Mrs. Fletcher. The other pupils started to clamber off after them.

'We can't follow Nate,' said Millie.

'We don't have much choice,' said Philip.

Miss Brown came up the aisle towards them, checking left and right to ensure no one had left anything behind. 'Hurry up, you two.'

Philip grabbed Millie's hand and pulled her towards the front. Millie eyed the open door and all of a sudden felt extremely reluctant to leave the safety of the bus. She didn't know what was going on out there, but she knew she didn't like it.

'Wait,' she said to Philip, trying to pull him back, 'This is what they *want* me to do...'

But now Miss Brown was coming up behind her, shepherding them along, and before Millie knew it she and Philip were outside and following the straggling line up the road, away from the snarled-up traffic, the well-dressed demonstrators and the animals. Without slackening his pace, Nate kept glancing back over his shoulder to scowl at Millie, as if to convey to her that this mess was all *her* fault.

It wasn't fair, she thought again, but couldn't help wondering if Nate was right. *Was* it her fault? Had this all happened because she'd forged her mother's signature? Could it be it karma? Or something worse?

Nate led them to one side of the Gare de l'Est and up a flight of steps. They could see railway lines to their right, but soon they were heading away from those tracks and along a rather sleazy-looking road where shabbily dressed men were hanging around smoking outside dimly lit bars.

Then they crossed a road and rounded a corner, and there in front of them was another big railway station, the Gare de Nord.

'Just in time for check-in!' said Miss Brown excitedly. 'Well done, Nate!'

Nate was too far away to hear the praise, but Millie could see Mrs. Fletcher slapping him on the back.

Nate, it seemed, was the hero of the hour.

Chapter 8
Operation Jackalope

Dupontel lit his tenth cigarette of the day and drew the smoke into his lungs in a convulsive spasm of annoyance. He had vastly exceeded his self-imposed quota, but these were testing times, and soon he would have to face Miss Pim and explain what had gone wrong, which was not something he was looking forward to.

He was surrounded by idiots, yet it was he, Dupontel, who would ultimately be held accountable for this fiasco, and he, Dupontel, who would be punished for it. He just hoped he wouldn't be struck off the list, after all the time and effort he'd put into ensuring his name was moving steadily towards the top of it.

The rabbit had as good as delivered herself into their clutches! Up until that morning, they'd had no idea where she was, or who she was, or if she *was* a she. No idea at all. They hadn't even been sure she wasn't a myth! But then, of her own free will, she had broken the seal and had all but placed herself in their grasp...

And they'd let her slip away.

Even now the school party was on its way back to St. Pancras, the train already racing across the flat fields of northern France and, short of dispatching a sabotage squad to derail it or blow up the tunnel - thus running the risk of losing the prize forever amid the inevitable carnage - there was nothing anyone could do.

And the bungling didn't stop there. Dupontel sighed and pressed the button on the intercom. 'You might as well send him in.'

He just had time to finish his cigarette and stub it out before the doors slid silently open, and Moreau was pushed into the room, so roughly that he fell to his knees. As the doors closed behind him he got to his feet, brushing himself down as though he'd fallen over on purpose. He was still wearing his waiter's uniform.

Dupontel sat down on the sofa. Moreau made a move towards one of the armchairs but Dupontel shook his head, so he remained standing. Dupontel let him stew for a while, fixing him with that unblinking glare he knew made his employees nervous. Then, in his best sorrowful tone, he asked, 'Tell me, Denis, what went wrong?'

Moreau tried to make himself smaller, but failed. 'We identified her correctly. It's not my fault Borowitz bungled the pick-up.'

'She found the Blood Pearl, Denis. You let her find the *Blood Pearl*.'

Moreau spread his hands. 'How did I know she'd want oysters? All those other kids were ordering chips. Have you ever known an English teenager want to eat oysters, Henri?'

'Dupontel to you, idiot! You should have made sure they were off the menu, for heaven's sake!'

'I had no say in the running of the place!' huffed Moreau. 'I was there on sufferance. The other waiters resented me! They said it was nepotism, and that I was getting all the best-tipping tables...'

'I do not give a fig about inter-waiter politics. I do give a fig, however, that not only did you have the rabbit in your grasp and allow her to escape, not only did you allow her to find the pearl and take it with her back to England, but now your bungling has left us with two unwanted and totally useless English teenagers on our hands. Have you any idea of the trouble this will cause? Not to mention the fact that the Arthurians now know that we know, and will henceforth be on maximum alert. *And* we're going to have to pay off the cops to stop them sniffing around in search of the missing kids. We'll never get another chance like the one we had today.'

Moreau shrugged. He was an expert shrugger. 'How was I to know they'd swap clothes?'

'Explain to me once again why you failed to go to the cemetery with Griffon and Borowitz to identify the target.'

'I couldn't leave. I hadn't finished my shift...'

Dupontel couldn't believe what he was hearing. 'And Becker? Verneuil? I suppose they have some equally pathetic excuse?'

"They had some sort of falling out, I have no idea what it was about, but you know what they're like. And then there was unexpected interference from Ramona and her stupid bird. I am not clear about the details; the Minister for Agriculture's under-secretary had just come into the brasserie with his mistress and I'd been ordered to give them special treatment.'

Dupontel rolled his eyes in exasperation. 'Ramona? You mean someone has already tipped off the Paris Chapter?'

Moreau risked another shrug. 'Who knows? Perhaps we have a mole in our ranks.' He looked hopeful, as though this could let him off the hook. 'Yes, I expect there's a mole.'

'Where are the two English children now? Please tell me they're still alive.'

''They're in the Voltaire basement.'

He flinched as Dupontel leapt to his feet and started yelling. ''The Voltaire basement! Are you crazy? They won't last two minutes down there after dark. What if we need them as hostages or bargaining chips? Is there no end to your idiocy?'

'It wasn't my decision,' said Moreau, but Dupontel was no longer listening. He stabbed the intercom button with his finger.

'Reeves? Is that you? Take the hostages out of the basement and up to the Grenier apartments, right now... Separately, yes of course, we don't want them putting their heads together and getting a message out. Yes, I know.... No, *immediately*. Well, get a bloody move on, then. If anything happens to them I will have your head... On a platter, yes. Oh, and send a runner here to pick up Moreau and escort him to the Crypt.'

At the word 'Crypt' Moreau's eyes opened wide with fear. 'Henri, it truly was not my fault. She was wearing the red scarf... I thought we were friends, Henri. Please don't do this...'

Dupontel rolled his eyes. 'You are a disgrace to Maison Pim. All that's left for you now is slake the thirst of the Council. I only hope I too will get off so lightly when it's my turn to face the music. And I will be *obliged* to face it - the infernal orchestra is tuning its instruments even as we speak.'

The runner arrived and took the trembling Moreau away.

Dupontel lit his eleventh cigarette of the day, and began mentally to rehearse what he could say to Miss

Pim that wouldn't necessarily end with her totally losing her temper and tearing his throat out.

*****

In contrast to the joyful energy that had filled the train on the way to Paris that morning, the mood on the return journey was sombre. A combination of fatigue and anxiety made everyone fractious, and several squabbles had broken out before they arrived at St. Pancras. A number of pupils made catty remarks to Millie, as though they blamed her personally for the disappearance of Paula and Sam, but for the most part they ignored her, as though, without Paula at her side, she was hardly worth noticing.

Now it was nearly midnight, and those who hadn't yet been dropped off were impatient to get home. Millie felt relief as the bus approached Ferret Lane. But the relief was mixed with anxiety. How could she greet her parents as though nothing had happened?

As she moved up to the front of the bus, Miss Brown tapped her on the shoulder. 'You'll be all right from here, Millie? Do you want me to walk you to your door?'

Millie glanced at the driver, who didn't look as though he relished the idea of loitering at the pick-up point any longer than was necessary. Like everyone else, he was eager to get home. He pressed a button and the doors slid open. Outside, Ferret Lane was the same as ever, flat and featureless, the gleam of the tarmac testifying to the rain that had fallen while they'd been away. The shapes of the hills to the north and east were silhouetted faintly against the night sky, with Cutter's

Peak, as usual, standing out like a cracked tooth. The Putnam farm was in darkness, but that was normal; Harvey and Martha Putnam always went to bed early, because they had to get up at the crack of dawn to feed the chickens and milk the cows. Somewhere in the trees to the south of the marshes, a nightjar trilled softly.

And yet... something had changed, Millie could feel it. The lane felt... different.

But she swallowed her nervousness. 'No, I'll be fine, thank you. It's only a couple of minutes' walk from here.'

It's only Boringwood, she thought. It's not as though I could ever be in any *danger* here.

'All right then, Millie, take care now.' Miss Brown patted her on the shoulder. 'Don't worry. Paula and Sam will be back tomorrow.'

Millie gave her a weak smile before turning back to the doors and stepping out - straight into a large puddle. She promptly hopped on to the muddy grass verge, but the damage was done - her trainers were sodden.

She turned to wave goodbye to Philip, but he was staring blankly at the back of the seat in front of him, like a witness to a terrible accident who had retreated, traumatised, into his shell.

As the bus moved off, one of its enormous wheels ploughed through the puddle Millie had already stepped in, and drenched the side of her jeans with dirty water. It felt like the last straw, a fitting end to an awful day.

She was a little surprised to find neither of her parents waiting at the pick-up point, before remembering she herself had told them she didn't know what time she'd be back, and that she would call during the day so they could come and meet her as usual. It had completely slipped her mind. Her stomach turned a small backflip. Had they phoned the school while she'd been away? Did they already know where she'd been? They would certainly be waiting up for her at the cottage, and now she had to face them, and pretend everything was normal.

Or did they already know what had happened?

She squelched towards the green, feeling like a prisoner who'd been on the run and was now about to give herself up. The disappearance of Paula and Sam was gnawing away at her inside; she couldn't possibly swan around with an idiotic grin on her face. Even if her parents hadn't learnt about the day's events, they would surely notice she was worried about something. Millie hadn't given much thought to what she was going to tell them, and now it was too late, because she felt too exhausted to come up with a convincing cover story.

Astronomy class! Of all the stupid fibs! She could think of a hundred more plausible excuses without even trying. She hoped her parents wouldn't have been wondering how one could possibly spend all day studying astronomy when the stars weren't even visible.

St. Leonard's was in darkness as she passed, which was a mercy, because at least it meant she wouldn't have to worry about Reverend Pardew spotting her from the annex window. She didn't know why, exactly, but the idea of him seeing her made her even more nervous, as though he would be able to peer right into her head and know everything that had happened, and that it had all been her fault, just as Nate had said.

Pardew and Nate were a well-matched pair, she thought with a shudder. They both hated her for no good reason.

As she rounded the corner by the church and saw the drab village green laid out in front of her, as boring as ever, a thick blanket of depression descended over her shoulders. She was trapped in Bramblewood, probably for the rest of her life. Today had only proved beyond a doubt that she couldn't escape, not even for a few hours, without something going horribly wrong. Even if her parents hadn't yet heard about Paula and Sam, there was no way they would ever let Millie out of their sight once they learnt what had happened. They wouldn't punish her. Not physically, anyway. They wouldn't be cruel, or even particularly angry; they just weren't like that. But they would be disappointed, she knew. And all trips to anywhere but school would be cancelled for the foreseeable future.

Nothing nice would ever happen to her again.

This was it, then. This was the end.

*****

The ducks drilled her with their sideways gaze as she passed the pond, and she automatically tensed, ready to have her eardrums pierced by the usual high-pitched whistling. But instead there was an eerie silence. She stared back at them. They were treading water listlessly; Millie wondered if their eyes had always looked that glassy, or if they were sick. Their plumage looked even drabber than usual. Maybe they were hungry; for the first time in her life she wondered who fed them, and what they ate, and resolved to throw them some breadcrumbs in the morning.

'What's the matter? Cat got your little ducky tongues?' she asked in a low voice, wondering as she said it if the ducks even had tongues.

The birds gave her what she interpreted as a look of disdain before turning their backs and paddling lethargically over to the far side of the pond. She wasn't sorry to see them go, but in her current mood it seemed as though they were deserting her. She pressed on towards her house, thankful to see that, like the church, it was in darkness. Her parents weren't waiting up for her, then. This was good news; it would give her time to come up with a cover story.

But as she drew nearer, she saw they hadn't even closed the curtains.

In fact, she saw now, all the houses were in darkness, not just hers. It seemed her parents weren't the only ones who had gone to bed early. Tanith's windows were dark, which was surprising as Tanith tended to stay up well past midnight. Dina and Perry Vaughan's place was unlit too, as was the house old Harold Jones shared with his slightly more sprightly cousin Mick. She turned to look back at the muddy green she'd just crossed. Was it her imagination or was the whole of Bramblewood unusually quiet this evening? Not that she was ever normally out this late, but she'd gazed out of her bedroom window often enough. It was never exactly Piccadilly Circus out there, but tonight it was different. Tonight it felt like a ghost town.

The path across the green was lit by the single lamp in the middle casting dull orangey-yellow stripes over the brown grass. The only other light was in the windows of the Bramblewood Arms, which were dimpled in a fake olde world effect, and as usual steamed up, so she couldn't see inside, and certainly not from this far away.

But only now did Millie register the uncanny silence. Maybe everyone was in the pub, but if so they weren't singing or even talking. Maybe her parents were in there too, but she didn't think it likely. The other villagers always greeted them respectfully, but Mr. and Mrs. Greenwood had never been the life and soul of the party.

Setting her misgivings aside, Millie reached her doorstep. Steeling herself for the inevitable confrontation, she inserted her key into the lock...

And found it already unlocked. Alarm bells immediately started ringing in her head. This was not right. Her parents would never leave the door unlocked at night, even though, as far as she knew, there had never been a single break-in or act of vandalism in the history of Bramblewood.

Making as little noise as possible she pushed the door all the way open and stepped inside, softly closing it behind her. She slipped out of her muddy trainers and, holding them by the shoelaces, tiptoed in stockinged feet down the hall towards the bottom of the staircase, her path lit by the filaments of colour refracted through the fanlight.

She knew she had to be extra careful, because some of the floorboards were creaky. She'd long ago learnt to identify their whereabouts in relation to the pattern on the carpet, not for any particular reason other than boredom, but she was grateful for that now. *This* one, she thought, carefully stepping over an ornate lily that seemed to be turning itself inside out. The lily pattern on the carpet was as familiar as old socks; there were variations of it all over the house, including in her own bedroom. She guessed her parents must have bought all the carpets at the same time, for a discount or something, probably before she was born.

And here: another flower. Stepping around it drew her level with the door to the living room, where she stopped.

The door was open, which once again was unusual, but it was what was *beyond* the door that made her pause.

There was something lying crumpled in a big heap on the floor in the middle of the room, just discernible in the dim lamplight filtering through the windows.

Millie stood there, trying to make sense of it. This was a major aberration. Her parents were preternaturally tidy. They *never* left things lying around, and especially not in the middle of the floor like that.

She took a step towards the heap, and stopped again, staring.

For a heart-stopping moment she'd thought it was a body sprawled on the floor.

No, *two* bodies.

Then, to her relief, saw it was just a heap of clothes. Or rather, two heaps: one a navy blue suit, the other a grey pleated skirt and white blouse with a pussycat bow and cultured pearl necklace. Her parents' clothes, in other words. Lying there, all spread out on the carpet, as though waiting for their owners to come downstairs and put them on.

Millie drew nearer to the clothes, circling them warily, and inadvertently nudged a navy blue trouser leg with her toe. It felt soft and crumbly, as though the leg bones inside it had been pulverised. But there was no one inside the trousers, she was sure of that. They were flat and empty.

Only then did she see that the clothes were covered in dust. In the dim light, it looked reddish.

No, not dust, too coarse for that. *Earth.*

The clothes, and the carpet around them were sprinkled with dry red earth. Crumbs of it were clinging to the toe of her sock. She moved back in surprise, dropping her trainers, hardly hearing the sharp crack of the floorboard as her stockinged heel came down on one of the flowers in the carpet.

This was unprecedented. Her parents would never leave clothes and dirt strewn all over the floor like this. The feel of that trouser leg when she'd touched it with her toe... She started to feel sick.

Millie wasn't sure how long she stood there, trying in vain to make sense of the empty clothes and the dirt spilling out of them, but her numbed reverie was shattered by the sound of screeching tyres outside. The room was lit up by red and blue lights flashing through the window, and she heard a slamming of car doors, and a babble of voices, followed by a mighty crash from the hallway behind her.

The front door.

She tried to think back, wondering if she'd forgotten to lock it behind her, but either way it was open now, and someone was coming through it, into the house. More than one of them, by the sound of it. There was a clatter of heavy shoes, followed by a battery of sharp cracks as several pairs of feet came down the hallway, trampling unheedingly over the flowers on the carpet.

It was almost as though the noisy floorboards had been placed there deliberately, Millie thought, as some sort of warning. Well, she felt duly warned. But too late now to look for a hiding place. She grabbed the poker from the hearth and turned to face the open doorway.

And saw an enormous dark figure. But it wasn't the size of the figure that worried her so much as the blazing yellow eyes, and the blood-red mouth, and the green sparks leaping from its fingers.

She tightened her grip on the poker.

'Miss Greenwood?'

Millie blinked. The figure dwindled and the sparks fizzled out, and she saw the eyes weren't blazing after all. An arm reached out to switch on the overhead light, and she saw it was just a normal-sized arm attached to a normal-sized man dressed in a navy blue overcoat. He seemed relieved to see her. There was still a lot of activity in the hallway behind him. The floorboards were crackling like a firework display. But the man's eyes swept the room with interest, taking in the piles of clothes on the floor before finally returning to Millie. He took a step towards her, holding out his hand for the poker, which she relinquished without argument. He passed it to someone behind him and held out his hand to her again.

'It's all right now, Miss Greenwood. I'm Detective Walker. Please come over here, and watch your step. We wouldn't want you treading in *that*.'

At the word *that*, an expression of distaste crossed his face. But Millie started back towards him, feeling relief, then anxiety, then relief all over again. The police were here; they would know what to do. They would find her parents, and everything would be all right.

Or would it? Halfway across the room, she paused to look at Detective Walker more carefully. He was making a huge effort to look friendly, but she noticed the smile didn't reach his eyes. He kept looking past her at the room, his glance moving from side to side, as though he were searching for something.

'Who called you?' asked Millie. 'Was it someone in the village? Did they tell you my name?'

Walker shook his head. 'Anonymous tip-off.'

A man in a lab coat brushed past her. She turned to see he had knelt down by the empty clothes and was intently spooning some of the red dust into a small plastic bag.

'Wait,' said Millie. 'I'm not sure you should be doing that.'

'We'd like to speak to your parents,' said Walker.

'So would I,' said Millie. 'But I don't think they're here.'

'When did you last see them?'

'This morning,' said Millie, panicking again. Perhaps this had something to do with Paula and Sam's disappearance. 'Why do you need to speak to them? Has this got something to do with what happened in Paris?'

Detective Walker shook his head again. 'I'd rather not go into that right now. Let's just say this involves your father's firm, and rather a large sum of money missing from accounts.'

Millie was flummoxed. 'What are you talking about?'

Walker sighed. 'I know it's hard for a young lady such as yourself to understand, but I'm afraid it looks as though your parents have gone on the run. They're criminals.'

'They're what?' Millie couldn't believe her ears.

Walker glanced at his watch. 'It's late. We can't let you stay here on your own, especially not after what happened to Paula O'Keefe and Samuel Tulliver.'

'What *did* happen to Paula and Sam?' asked Millie, suddenly suspicious. 'Do you know where they are?'

Instead of responding to her questions, Walker turned and made a sign with his hand. A stern-looking middle-aged woman came bustling up in an authoritative manner.

'This is Miss Cameron. She'll be looking after you till the courts decide what to do with you.'

'What do you mean?' Millie said. 'I live here. You can't just take me away like that...'

'You're under eighteen,' said Miss Cameron. 'You can't stay here on your own. You need to come with us.' She gripped Millie firmly by the arm.

'What did the Paris police say?' Millie persisted. 'Have they found Paula and Sam?'

Walker looked impatient. 'Look, we don't have time for this right now. We need to get you out of here as soon as possible, before...'

'Now hold on,' said Millie, planting her heels in the pile of the carpet. For an odd moment, it felt as though one of her feet was stuck; she glanced down and saw - or thought she saw - one of the tendrils from the pattern in the carpet had escaped from its mooring and had wound itself around her ankle. Which of course was impossible. She shook her head violently and the impression vanished. It was just a normal carpet covered in an elaborate flower pattern.

'Now don't be difficult, Millie,' said Cameron. 'You're already in enough trouble as it is.'

It flashed through Millie's head that she was being arrested. Probably for forging her mother's signature.

Then she thought *no!* That was ridiculous; something else was going on here. But she could feel herself being dragged by Miss Cameron, inch by inch towards the hall. As they reached the doorway she grabbed the frame and clung on to it for dear life.

'I want to make a phone call! You can't stop me doing that.'

'You can call from the station,' said Walker.

Millie racked her brains, trying to remember what happened in TV crime shows.

'Show me your badge!'

'My badge?' said Walker, exasperated. 'If you insist, Millie. But I fear this pointless attempt at insubordination is only going to...' He began to reach into his inside pocket.

'Hold it right there!' said a voice from the hallway.

Millie felt her knees go weak with relief. Tanith! Her aunt was shouldering her way through the wedge of policemen in the hall. Just visible behind her, peering in through the front door, were the anxious faces of Mrs. Crumley, Dr. Scott and Mr. Figgs. Millie had never felt so happy to see them in her life.

Tanith smiled at Millie as she stepped forward into the room, but her smile was clouded with worry. 'Hello, Millie. Good to see you.'

Miss Cameron dropped Millie's arm and backed towards Detective Walker.

Tanith's eyes flew around the room and took in the entire scene before coming to rest on Walker. 'It's OK, you can leave now. Millie will be staying with me from now on.'

'You have no right...' said Miss Cameron.

'I have *every* right,' said Tanith. 'As I am sure you are already well aware, in the absence of Millie Greenwood's parents I am her legal guardian. I can show you the papers, if you insist.'

'We're investigating a disappearance. Four disappearances, in fact,' said Walker, puffing his chest out. But Tanith's arrival had taken the wind out of his sails.

'Maybe you are,' said Tanith, before adding, cryptically, 'and maybe you aren't. Either way, you have no right to interview Millie without a parent or guardian present. And you certainly have no right to turn up in the middle of the night and kidnap her. I think you'll have a hard time coming up with official paperwork for that.'

Kidnap? Millie's head was buzzing with questions. What was this? International Kidnap Millie Greenwood Day? She looked inquiringly at Tanith, but her aunt's attention was fixed on Walker and Cameron as they sidled out of the room, as though she didn't dare take her eyes off them for a second.

'You too, Mr. CSI,' she said to the man on his knees, still busily collecting samples of the red dust. 'You can drop the charade, as well as those packets you've already collected... Yes, including that one you just slipped into your pocket.'

The man dropped his packets, stumbled apologetically to his feet and followed Walker and Cameron out of the room. Tanith crossed to the window and watched them climb into one of the two police cars. The big men from the hallway got into the other car. Tanith kept watching as both engines started up, and the cars slowly rolled around The Noose and disappeared down Ferret Lane.

She exhaled, as though she'd been holding her breath for a very long time, and turned back to Millie, enveloping her in a hug so tight it threatened to crush her ribs.

'Come next door, and I'll make you a cup of tea, and you can tell me where you've been.'

Millie jammed her wet trainers back on to her feet and, with just one backward glance at the crumpled clothes on the floor, allowed herself be led towards the front door. She was thankful to see Tanith after the weirdness of the past few minutes, but her head was buzzing with so many questions that, for once, anxiety over the forged signature was relegated to second place.

What had happened to her parents? Why had they left the house in such disarray? And what on earth would they say when they found out about the trip to Paris? Her secret was out in the open now - even the detective had known, even if he hadn't wanted to discuss it. And if Tanith didn't know about it, she soon would. Her aunt meant business, she could tell, and Millie didn't feel capable of responding to any direct questioning with barefaced lies.

Oh, and who had called the police?

She voiced the small suspicion that had been niggling away at the back of her mind ever since she'd first laid eyes on Walker.

'Were they really police?'

'I'm afraid so, yes,' said Tanith. 'But the Old Bill, like every other institution, can be both good and bad, and those guys were some of the rotten apples. Let's just be grateful I got here when I did.'

She led Millie outside, where Mrs. Crumley let out a little cry and gave her a hug almost as suffocating as Tanith's had been. 'Millie! Thank goodness! We thought you'd been taken.' Dr. Scott and Mr. Figgs looked shaken but relieved.

'I saw clouds,' said Mrs. Crumley, 'but not what they were concealing. Sometimes I wonder what the point is of seeing anything at all.'

Dr. Scott patted her on the arm. 'Don't be hard on yourself. You saw enough to put us on alert.'

'It was only thanks to you we got here in time,' said Mr. Figgs. 'I never imagined they could have sent someone over so quickly.'

'They were already here,' said Tanith. 'The Syndicate has installed sleeper agents all around the world, and not just because of Millie. It's how they operate.'

Mrs. Crumley asked Tanith if there was anything they could do.

'No, I've got this,' said Tanith. 'We'll talk in the morning.'

Mrs. Crumley, Dr. Scott and Mr. Figgs smiled shakily, nodded to one another and, without another word, turned and started back towards the Bramblewood Arms, where a small knot of people was gathered around the entrance, waiting for their return. Millie squinted to try and see them more clearly, but the light from the pub cast the figures into silhouette. Some appeared to be holding pint mugs and cigarettes. She had the impression that most of the village was gathered there.

Mrs. Crumley waved and shouted, 'She's OK! But the Greenwoods have gone, which puts the kibosh on Cottontail. We need to switch to Operation Jackalope.'

'Gone where?' asked Millie, vaguely wondering why Mrs. Crumley was talking gibberish. It wasn't Kidnap Millie Greenwood Day after all, she decided, it was Befuddle Millie Greenwood Day.

Some of the silhouettes outside the pub nodded and started shuffling back inside, but an extra-tall one with tattered sleeves stood his ground. Reverend Pardew, thought Millie, no more thrilled to see him than she ever was. But she was surprised to see him there; hanging out in the pub with the other villagers wasn't typical Pardew behaviour. He tended to keep himself to himself, and no one was in a hurry to tempt him out of his self-imposed isolation.

By now Mrs. Crumley was halfway across the green with her back to the cottages; her voice sounded muffled, but Millie could still make out the words.

'I said *Jackalope*, James.'

'I know what you said.' The voice of the Reverend boomed across the green. Obviously he had no need of church acoustics to make himself audible. 'And I still say *Myxomatosis*.'

Millie heard Tanith inhale sharply, and felt her aunt's hand tighten around hers.

'Come on Millie. I don't know about you, but I'm dying for that cup of tea.'

Tanith took Millie into her home, leaving Reverend Pardew and his tattered sleeves silhouetted against the light spilling out of the Bramblewood Arms.

Chapter 9
A Sliver of Quartz

The first thing Paula saw when she opened her eyes was a spider the size of a saucer, scuttling across a wall only a few inches from her face. She let out a shriek and leapt to her feet, cracking her head against something she realised, too late, was a low ceiling that felt as though it had been hewn out of solid rock.

Only then did she realise that she wasn't in her bedroom at home. She rubbed her head, which had been throbbing even before she'd banged it. Wherever she was, it was cold, and dark, and smelt of damp. Her jacket was covered in cobwebs and grime. This was not normal, she thought. Not normal at all.

'Welcome back to the land of the living,' a voice whispered into her ear. 'Watch your head on the ceiling. Come over here; there's more room.'

She turned, half-crouching, and saw a pale face hovering in the gloom. Sam. His expression was pinched; he looked almost as frightened as Paula felt.

She edged forward, trying to make sense of the semi-darkness, which seemed to be playing tricks with her depth perception. There was just enough light to make out shape and mass and movement, but not enough to fill in the details. After a few steps her hands connected with a rough surface. She explored it with her fingers, shuddering as they brushed against the sticky threads of what could only be more cobwebs. A stone wall. She turned and shuffled in the opposite direction; this time her progress was blocked by a line of rough wooden planks wired together.

'What the hell is this?' she asked. 'A *stockade?*'

'Some sort of cellar,' said Sam. 'There's the door. Padlocked on the other side.'

Paula's eyes were beginning to get used to the murk. After a lot of blinking and craning she finally detected the sole light source: a bright pinprick, a long way over their heads. It might have been a skylight, or maybe just a hole. Tipping her head back to stare at it made her neck ache, but as she lowered her chin she glimpsed something behind Sam. Something moving: a darker shape against the darkness.

Paula gasped and jerked back so abruptly that she banged her head on the ceiling again.

'It's OK, I don't bite,' said a voice with a heavy French accent. 'At least, not yet.'

'Sorry,' said Sam. 'Should have warned you: we're not the only ones here. This is Daniel.'

As Paula grew ever more accustomed to the gloom, she saw that Daniel was dressed in jeans and an old leather jacket and looked younger than her and Sam, though not by much.

'Pleased to meet you,' he said. 'I'm sorry it couldn't be in more agreeable circumstances.'

'Who are you?'

'A prisoner, like you.'

'Hang on,' said Paula, rubbing her head. 'Let's get this straight. Last thing I remember was the brasserie. Millie found something... A pearl! Then... No, it's all a blank! Are we still in Paris?'

'All I know is my head hurts,' said Sam.

Paula turned to the padlocked door in the wooden palings and raised her voice. 'Hello? Is there anyone there? HELLO?' She tried to rap on the wood, but the blow made barely a sound and she only succeeded in tenderising the side of her fist.

'Shush,' said Daniel. 'You don't want to attract their attention.'

'Oh, but I do,' said Paula. 'Hello? HELLO! LET US OUT OF HERE RIGHT NOW OR I'LL CALL THE COPS!'

'Oh yes?' said Sam. 'With what?'

Paula looked around for her bag, but it was nowhere to be seen. She checked her pockets. Her phone had gone too. 'Have we been mugged?'

'Kidnapped, I think,' said Sam.

'Where's Millie? Is she here?'

'Just the three of us,' said Sam.

'This is outrageous,' said Paula. She tried to stoke the anger bubbling up inside her, because it shunted the fear to one side. 'They can't keep us here. It's against the law!'

'They *are* the law,' said Daniel. 'They do what they please, and no one can stop them.'

'Wait,' said Paula. 'Have we been *arrested?*'

'Not by police,' said Sam. 'It's... oh, I don't know. But do you remember Millie telling us a waiter tried to kidnap her? Everyone thought she was making it up, but maybe...'

Paula rubbed her head. 'It's all so fuzzy, I can only remember bits and pieces... That stupid cemetery! I wish we'd never gone there. Did someone spike our drinks?'

'I remember Jim Morrison's tomb,' said Sam. "Then there was a...' He rubbed his face as though trying to summon a memory, or possibly erase it. 'Was Millie there? I can't remember. No idea. I woke up just before you did. But I do remember thinking your perfume was too strong.'

'I didn't put any on today,' said Paula.

'Maison Pim No. 5,' said Daniel. 'Smells divine, knocks you out cold. The drudges' usual cosh. Does your head hurt?'

'And how,' said Sam. 'Doesn't help that I keep banging it on the ceiling. This place must have built for midgets.'

'Who kidnapped us?' asked Paula. 'Slave traders?'

Daniel shook his head. 'Worse.'

Paula's eyes opened wide. 'What could be worse?'

'You're new to this, aren't you,' sighed Daniel. "Trust me, you wouldn't believe me if I told you.' He took out a battered packet of cigarettes and held it out to Paula and Sam, who both declined the offer. In the brief flare as Daniel struck a match, Paula saw a slender, good-looking boy with dark skin, and silky black hair drawn back into a ponytail. He drew on his cigarette and blew out a small cloud of smoke that looked blue in the darkness.

'I wish you wouldn't,' said Paula. 'It pollutes my airspace, and heaven knows there isn't a lot of that right now.'

Daniel took no notice, and carried on smoking.

Paul peered round the small dark space, her eyes straining to penetrate the shadows. 'What if I need to go to the toilet?'

'Bucket in the corner over there,' said Sam. 'It's OK, we won't look. But be careful not to knock it over.'

'Oh, this is ridiculous,' said Paula. She tried not to hyperventilate. 'I get claustrophobia. I think I'm going to have a panic attack.'

'Try to stay calm,' said Daniel. 'Someone's coming to help us.'

'Soon, I hope,' said Sam.

'Before it gets dark,' said Daniel, squinting up at the pinprick above them. 'At least I hope so. Or we're in big trouble.'

Paula followed his gaze upwards. Was it her imagination or had the light already dimmed?

'What happens when it gets dark?'

Daniel laughed mirthlessly. 'That's when they come out.' He dropped what remained of his cigarette and ground it out with his heel.

'Who's they?' asked Sam.

Daniel ignored the question. 'You're English, right? You're the ones who came by train this morning?'

'Yes, and there'll be someone looking for us,' said Paula. 'They can't just kidnap people off the street like that.'

'It wasn't a street,' said Sam.

Daniel shook his head. 'They can do whatever they like,' he said again. 'You have no idea what they're capable of. We just have to try and get away before they send someone down to get us.'

There was a soft pattering noise. Sam felt something scuttle over his foot and let out a yell. Paula looked down, and grabbed his arm.

A large brown rat. *Very* large, almost the size of a cat. It sat back on its hind legs and looked up at them inquiringly. Attached to a thong around its neck was a small leather pouch.

'Oh my god,' said Paula, trying to keep Sam between her and the giant rodent.

'Relax,' said Daniel. 'It's only Claudine.'

Paula and Sam exchanged a quick glance. They were already wary of their new companion, and now here he was, giving names to rats.

'How long have you been locked up here?' asked Paula.

'Since this morning, when they caught me tampering with one of their computers. And just as well I did, or they would have been at the railway station to meet you when the train got in... Salut, Claudine!'

Then something happened that made Paula and Sam wonder if they'd banged their heads even harder than they'd realised.

Through the half-light, they saw the rat twist and turn, this way and that, as though trying to shake off something that was clinging to its back. They shrank back as far as they could, which wasn't very far. As they watched, scarcely believing their eyes, the rat seemed to be balancing on its hind legs. And now its limbs were getting longer, and the fur on its back was rippling and getting thinner.

Paula jammed her hand over her mouth to stifle the scream that threatened to burst forth. Sam didn't trust himself to speak. The rat kept growing. With a flick of its paw, it loosened the thong around its neck and then it was twisting and changing until it was almost as tall as they were, and its fur had vanished.

The rat straightened up, and they saw it wasn't a rat at all, but a girl, nut-brown and completely naked apart from the pouch hanging from her neck. Her lack of clothing didn't seem to embarrass her. She dipped forward to kiss Daniel on both cheeks.

'Salut, Daniel,' she said, then gabbled something very fast, in French.

'They're English,' said Daniel. 'Is there any way we can take them with us?'

Claudine turned to look at Paula and Sam. Her stare was defiant, and a bit scornful. 'Can they shift?'

'I have no idea,' said Daniel. 'We only just met.'

'Wait,' said Paula. 'What just happened?'

She found it hard to stop staring at Claudine, not because she wasn't wearing any clothes, but because only a few moments ago the girl had been on all fours, covered in fur, with a long tail.

Sam sat down, heavily, on the ground. 'That... What did you call it? Pim No. 5? Does it cause hallucinations?'

Claudine sighed impatiently. 'We don't have time for persiflage. Daylight's almost gone. We'll have to leave them here, Dan.'

Paula promptly shelved all the questions she wanted to ask and came to a rapid decision. 'Please take us with you.'

These people were odd, and heaven knows what had just happened was unimaginably weird, but Paula's instinct told her to trust them. Besides, she was prepared to do just about anything to get out of this damp cellar.

Claudine turned to her and asked, 'Can you shift?'

Paula stared back at her, dumbstruck.

'They don't know what you're talking about,' said Daniel.

'Then I'm sorry, there's nothing we can do.' Claudine seemed genuinely regretful. 'We already have enough on our plate saving our own skins. You know what they do to people like us.' She gave Daniel a bleak look.

'No, wait,' said Daniel. He grabbed Paula's hand, and then one of Sam's, compelling them to focus on what he was saying. 'Look, we don't have much time. I'm going to say something that won't make much sense, but if you want to get out of here you'll just have to trust me, and listen. Claudine is a shapeshifter, Third Grade, which is fairly advanced. She can already change into small animals, like that rat you saw, and she doesn't need pills. I'm still only First Grade, which means I can only change into minerals, stones and crystals, basic things like that, and I still need a dose of moddy to morph back again. You're from that school, Mallory Hall, right? That means your family was handpicked, even if they don't know it, so there's an outside chance... If there were shifters anywhere in your ancestry, even hundreds of years ago, you'll carry the genes and maybe you can change too. A pebble would do, the smaller and simpler the better. Then Claudine can put us in her pouch and carry us out of here.'

Paula couldn't hold it in any longer.

'ARE YOU INSANE?'

'It's no good,' Claudine said to Daniel. 'Even if they have the genes, we don't have time to teach them.'

'We fell down a rabbit hole,' said Sam.

'Listen,' Daniel said again, speaking to Sam and Paula slowly and clearly, as though they were small children, and he was telling them how to cross the road safely. 'You've been kidnapped by some very bad people who work for a bunch of vampires. Once night has fallen, the vampires will come down here and they will probably drink your blood. If you're lucky, they'll kill you. If not, you'll become like them, and you'll end up doing awful things, things you would never have dreamt of, even in your worst nightmares. Believe me, you won't be happy. Your only hope is to turn yourself into a stone, and let Claudine carry you out with her. It's the only way you can get out of here.'

Paula's mouth fell open. Sam burst out laughing. 'This is crazy. But hey, it's already a bad dream, so I might as well give it a try. Come on then, how do I turn myself into a stone?'

Paula shook her head, also laughing, but there was an edge of hysteria to her voice. 'This has to be some sort of stupid prank. It's Nate McIntyre, isn't it. I don't know how, but he's punking us.'

Daniel didn't laugh. He held out a hand; nestling in the palm were three green capsules. 'These are push-pills. They won't do all the work for you, but they'll give you a nudge in the right direction. You'll need help to de-morph, but Claudine will take us back to the Academy, and there are professors there who can... She knows who to trust.'

Sam laughed again and took one of the pills between his thumb and forefinger. 'This is like *The Matrix*... Nah, it's even weirder than that. Here goes.'

'Oh, I don't believe it,' said Paula. 'Sam, you can't... You have no idea what that is.'

'Look at it this way,' said Sam, 'Things can't get much worse.' And he popped the pill in his mouth and swallowed. 'Now what?'

Daniel muttered something in a language they didn't understand, but it didn't sound to them like French. He popped one of the two remaining pills into his own mouth and offered the last one to Paula.

Reluctantly, she took it and said, 'Cheers!' before putting it in her mouth and swallowing. She didn't have much saliva so it got stuck in her throat, so she had to gulp, several times, to force it down as Daniel muttered something in the unknown language again.

'OK, now here's the tricky part. Close your eyes. You need to think of a stone or pebble. The smaller the better. Picture it in your mind, something very basic. Imagine you're touching it; feel its surface. Can you see it?'

Sam closed his eyes. 'I'm thinking about a stone I threw into the river a few weeks ago. It's very smooth and flat. Grey. It skipped over the surface of the water.'

'That's the idea,' said Daniel. 'Keep concentrating on it. How about you? I'm sorry, what was your name?'

'Paula.'

'Close your eyes, Paula.'

'I'm a pebble,' she said, closing her eyes but almost immediately opening them again. 'Who am I kidding? I'm not a pebble! This is nuts.'

'Have a go,' urged Sam. 'What have you got to lose?'

Paula bit her lip, closed her eyes again, and tried to concentrate. All of a sudden, the ground seemed to fall away. There were whispering sounds all around her. Somewhere in the distance, a door slammed. She could smell damp, and a faint whiff of garlic. Molecules of the champagne she'd tasted at lunchtime danced in her mouth.

'I'm that smooth oval pebble I found on the beach in the Algarve last year,' she whispered. 'It has a streak of pink running through it...'

'No!' said Claudine. 'Forget the pink! Much too complicated for a beginner.'

Paula tried to imagine the pebble without the pink streak, but she couldn't help it; the colour kept coming back. Claudine said, 'Hurry up!' which didn't help.

'You are the essence of that stone,' said Daniel. 'Imagine you *are* the stone.'

Paula heard Sam murmuring, 'OK, I am the stone. I am the stone. I am the...'

His voice faded away. Paula opened her eyes. Sam was gone. Claudine let out a little gasp and clapped her hands. 'Oh my God, he did it! He actually did it! Amazing!'

'Where is he?' said Paula, looking around. Was Sam hiding from them? But there was nowhere to hide in the tiny cellar. There had barely been enough space for the four of them.

Daniel dipped down to pick something up. When he straightened up there was a flat grey stone in the palm of his hand. 'He did it, first time! Honestly, I didn't expect that. Almost as if he'd done it before.' He loosened the opening of the pouch around Claudine's neck and dropped the stone into it. 'Pity he couldn't have made himself a bit smaller. Will he be too heavy for you?'

'I'll be fine,' said Claudine. 'Marius and Zahia are waiting across the street.'

'Now your turn,' Daniel said to Paula.

'Where's Sam? What have you done with him?'

'I'm sorry,' said Claudine. 'I know this must all seem very strange to you. But we have to get a move on. Listen!'

From somewhere far above their heads came sounds of activity. A door slammed, then another, and then there were scattered footsteps, and a crash, some sort of electronic mechanism whirring into life, muffled clanking. And faint laughter, like the sound of guests enjoying themselves at a distant cocktail party.

'They're coming for us!' said Claudine.

'Come on, Paula,' said Daniel. 'You can do it.'

'I want Sam,' said Paula. 'Where is he? I want to go home.'

Daniel grabbed her hand again and squeezed it. Paula squeezed back, grateful for the human contact.

'Come on,' he said. 'Try and think about that pebble again. It's your only chance.'

'We're running out of time,' said Claudine. 'I can't let them catch me here again.'

For the first time, her defiant demeanour wavered. The fear in her voice frightened Paula more than anything that had happened. Tears welled up in her eyes. She squeezed them shut and once again tried to imagine herself as a pebble, this time without the pink streak, but the mental image kept floating further and further away. The whole idea was just too preposterous. When it was clear nothing was going to happen, she gave up and opened her eyes.

'Please bring Sam back. Please.'

'We can't,' said Claudine. 'Not here.'

Daniel stroked Paula's hand sympathetically. 'I'm sorry, we really do have to go. I don't want to leave you, but we don't have a choice. Your boyfriend will be safe with us. We'll send someone back to get you.'

'He's not my boyfriend,' said Paula, then bit her tongue. Because what did it matter, when the mechanical clanking and the laughter were getting closer?

Daniel and Claudine exchanged looks. Paula saw the terror in their faces, made up her mind, and took a deep breath. 'Hey, you go on without me. I'll be OK. I'll talk my way out of it. I've talked my way out of situations worse than this.'

'I'm so sorry,' said Daniel. 'Believe me, if there was anything more we could do, we would do it.'

'Let's go!' said Claudine, increasingly nervous.

Daniel kissed Paula on both cheeks. 'Goodbye then, Paula. Be brave. I really hope we meet again.'

'You can count on it,' said Paula, trying to sound more cheerful than she felt. He really was good-looking, she thought. And charming too, even if he was younger than her usual crushes. Such a pity there was no time to get to know him better.

But, she thought, *at least I can leave him with a last impression of me that isn't all runny-nosed and semi-hysterical.* So she swallowed the pesky lump in her throat, summoned her most confident smile, and said, as lightheartedly as she could, 'We *will* meet again, I promise. You can't shake me off that easily!'

Daniel gazed into her eyes intently, and sighed, and for a second she thought he was going to announce that he would stay behind with her after all. But then he muttered something in the strange language.

And, just like that, he was gone.

Claudine stooped and picked up something. Paula glimpsed a small sliver of quartz, which the rat-girl popped into her pouch. Paula heard a soft chink as it joined the pebble already in there. *Sam.* Could that *really* be Sam in there? She had to be dreaming. There was no other rational explanation for what had happened.

Claudine took Paula's face between her hands and stared directly into her eyes. Paula was surprised, and touched, to see the other girl's face was wet with tears.

'Be brave, English girl. We will avenge you.'

Her compassionate expression made Paula want to burst into tears as well, but she just managed to hold them in. And then suddenly she was on her own. She looked down and suppressed a shriek as the brown rat reared up on its hind legs and waggled a paw at her before securing the pouch around its neck. It was a lot heavier than before, and the thong dragged at its fur, but then the animal was down on all fours and squeezing through a gap between the wooden palings, the contents of the pouch making a faint clinking sound as the rodent scuttled off into the darkness on the other side.

Paula stared after the rat.

This has to be the strangest dream I've ever had, she thought. *I expect I'll wake up any minute now.*

But she didn't wake up. She shut her eyes again and tried to think of rainbows and kittens, but all she could hear now was the ominous mechanical clanking growing louder and louder... Until it stopped, and there was an ugly metallic screeching that set Paula's teeth on edge, and more laughter, and several sets of footsteps, coming closer...

The footsteps stopped on the other side of the door, and there was a shuffling and Paula heard the jingle of keys, and someone said, 'Let's see what's on the menu, shall we.'

Chapter 10
The Dolls

In her looking-glass version of the Greenwoods' house, Tanith swapped Millie's wet trainers for slippers and settled her on the sofa, which looked like a threadbare antique but was really rather comfortable. Then she added a log to the fire and prodded at it with the poker until small tongues of flames revived and started licking at the wood. Millie was feeling a bit shivery, so was grateful for the extra warmth. She was aching with fatigue as well, but knew that until she could make some sort of sense out of what was going on, sleep would be out of the question.

Tanith leaned over to gaze anxiously into her eyes, as though trying to find the answer to a riddle there. 'All right, Millie?'

'I think so. But I don't understand. Where are my mother and father?'

'All in good time,' said Tanith. 'We're going to have to take this slowly, I think. First let me go and put the kettle on. You look as though you could do with a sandwich. And I do believe I have some ginger biscuits somewhere. Maybe even almond crunchies.'

Millie realised she was indeed feeling peckish. Some of the other pupils had bought sandwiches on the journey home, but Millie hadn't much felt like eating until now.

While Tanith busied herself in the kitchen, Millie gazed into the flickering fire and tried once again to work out where she had gone wrong. It wasn't so hard. If only she hadn't forged that signature. If only she hadn't wanted to go to Paris so very, very badly. But was it really her fault? Her parents were overprotective, she knew that much. They couldn't expect her to stay cooped up for ever. Maybe if they'd been less strict with her, all this would never have happened, and Paula and Sam would never have gone missing.

On the other hand, Paula and Sam had snuck off to be on their own together, behind Millie's back, so perhaps some of it was their fault too...

She shook this nonsense out of her head. There was no point in trying to find someone to blame. Just because Paula and Sam had been kissing didn't mean they deserved to be kidnapped. Because now she was absolutely sure that was what had happened. Paula had been wearing Millie's red scarf in the cemetery. Ergo, the kidnappers had mistaken her for Millie.

But why would anyone want to kidnap *her?* She thought back to the creepy waiter's bungled attempt at the restaurant, and shuddered. That had been just after...

Just after she'd found the pearl. It had to have something to do with the pearl. Her eyes filled with tears. Well, in that case why hadn't he just asked for it? She would gladly have given it up in return for Paula and Sam. It was only a stupid ugly pearl. Not worth anyone getting kidnapped over.

If Paula and Sam weren't back at school the next day - and she hoped with all her might that they would be - perhaps she could offer the pearl as ransom. Stupid pearl. She wished she'd never found it. Why on earth had she ordered oysters? Why hadn't she stuck to steak and chips, like everyone else? Had she just been showing off, after all?

Tanith came back in with a teapot, mugs and food on a wooden tray which she set down on the low table between the sofa and armchairs.

'Tuck in,' she said.

Millie helped herself to a ham and cheese sandwich. It looked like a regular sandwich, but Millie wondered what else Tanith had put in it, because it turned out to be the most delicious thing she'd ever tasted.

Tanith poured out the tea. It wasn't fancy tea this time - just regular English breakfast tea, with milk. Then she leant back in her armchair, and steepled her fingers in a curiously ceremonial manner. 'We have a lot to talk about.'

Millie paused halfway through her sandwich and sighed. 'Something awful happened today, and I'm afraid it was all my fault.'

Tanith raised her eyebrows. 'At school?'

Millie suspected Tanith knew perfectly well she hadn't been to school, but she didn't seem cross, just anxious. Millie thought she could detect a trace of wry amusement in there as well, and it was this that encouraged her to say what she said next.

'I, er, went on the class trip to Paris. I know I wasn't supposed to, but...'

And it all came spilling out, everything from the forging of the signature onwards. When she described her fainting fit in the Channel Tunnel, Tanith nodded solemnly and made a face, almost as though she was feeling the same pain as Millie had. And when Millie rather embarrassedly mentioned her strange impression that some of the statues and paintings in the Louvre had been watching her, Tanith nodded again, as though her theories were being confirmed.

When she got to the part about the brasserie, Millie fished around in the pocket of her backpack until her fingers closed on the now familiar lumpy shape. She peeled back the layers of tissue to show Tanith the pearl. It gleamed dully in the firelight, half-red, half-green.

Tanith's mouth fell open. Millie had never seen her so impressed. Her aunt reached out to touch the pearl, gingerly, as though expecting it to burst like a bubble on contact with her fingertip. 'So the stories are true.' She stared in silence at the pearl for half a minute before folding the tissue back over it and pressing it into Millie's hand. 'You keep that safe. It's yours now. And it's very special.'

'I was thinking of selling it on eBay,' said Millie, and chuckled at her aunt's horrified expression. 'Just kidding! But you'll have to tell me what's so special about it. Apart from me finding it in the middle of an oyster in the middle of lunch, I mean. I know you don't just find pearls like that. It doesn't happen.'

Tanith shook her head. 'Later. I'll tell you everything I know. But I'm afraid it's not much. For everyone's safety, we've all been operating on a need-to-know basis.'

'You make it sound like a spy thriller,' said Millie, suddenly excited. Maybe Bramblewood wasn't as boring as she thought. 'Don't tell me you're a secret agent.'

'It *is* a bit like a spy story, yes,' said Tanith. 'A game of smoke and mirrors - sometimes literally so. But we'll come to that. There's so much to tell you, but we'll have to deal with it bit by bit, otherwise you won't be able to take it all in without your head exploding... No, don't look so worried, it won't actually explode; that really is just a figure of speech... What happened after you found the pearl? I'm guessing that's when things started to turn really weird.'

Millie continued her story of the day's events. The more she talked, the better she felt. It was a relief to confide in Tanith. She only wished she'd done it earlier, before the Paris trip. Her aunt would surely have understood, just as she seemed to understand now.

'Zoo animals, you say?' said Tanith, as though it was the most natural thing in the world to see rhinos and zebras roaming the streets of Paris.

'Yes, and protesters too, only they all seemed to be wearing business suits or ballgowns.'

Tanith chuckled. 'Ah, Maison Pim. They always did have trouble dressing like regular folk.'

'Maison Pim? The designer label? What have they got to do with it?'

'Don't worry, we'll get to them soon enough. I'm sorry, I interrupted you...'

Millie finished her story, describing how she'd got home to find the empty clothes on the floor of the living room, and how Detective Walker had tried to take her away.

'And then you turned up.' Millie realised she was still hungry, so helped herself to another sandwich and wolfed it down in a couple of bites.

Tanith sipped her tea thoughtfully before setting the cup down and fixing Millie with another of her intense but kindly gazes. 'The first thing you should know, Millie, is that I'm not cross, not cross at all, about you slipping off to Paris. I knew something like this would happen, sooner or later. In fact, I warned them, but they wouldn't listen. No one's a spring chicken around here, as if you hadn't already noticed, and I think that having to cope with all the grey hair and wrinkles and arthritis has actually made them forget what it's like to be young. But I knew you would find some way of escaping before long. I'm not saying it was *right* to forge that signature, but I'd probably have done the same thing if I'd been in your shoes. In fact, I'm quite proud of you for taking the initiative and busting out of the stalag the way you did today. It's not your fault things went wrong. In fact, it's probably ours; we should have let you in on the secret a long time ago. But, as I said, some of us hadn't noticed that you were no longer a child. Well, we all underestimated you, and I'm terribly sorry about that.'

Millie felt a small explosion of pride, mixed with embarrassment.

Tanith leaned over and took her hand, and said, 'The first thing you need to know is that Marcus and Aurelia were not your real parents.'

Millie felt as though someone had pushed her off the edge of a very high cliff. She was falling, twisting and turning as the air rushed past her ears... and she felt like screaming...

But screaming in triumph. *I knew it!* Somewhere inside her, she'd always suspected those cold, distant people had not been her real parents. How could she ever have imagined they were? Trying not to let the excitement show in her face, Millie asked, 'Who are my real parents, then? And where are...' She realised she wasn't sure what to call them now. Then something Tanith had said belatedly sank in.

Marcus and Aurelia were not your real parents. Tanith had used the past tense.

'Are they all right? Marcus and Aurelia, I mean. I wouldn't want anything to happen to them, even if they aren't my real mum and dad.'

Tanith smiled, as if knowing perfectly well that Millie hadn't been entirely sorry to hear this news. 'It's OK, they've just gone back to where they came from. And you know I'm not your real aunt, not in the biological sense? I *am* your legal guardian, though. I didn't lie to the police about that.'

This time, Millie felt a twinge of disappointment at the news that she and Tanith weren't related by blood.

Tanith stood up. 'I've got a lot of explaining to do, and it'll probably take forever, but I think the best thing is to let you see some of it for yourself. You're too excited to sleep, right? So we have time for a bedtime story, at least.'

She motioned to Millie. Grabbing a fistful of biscuits for dessert, Millie followed her out into the hallway and up the stairs. Tanith stopped outside what Millie knew was the guest room and put her hand on the doorknob, and Millie's heart sank. She knew what was inside.

The dolls.

'This may seem quite frightening at first, Millie, but just remember - nothing you see in this room can possibly harm you.' She seemed to be weighing up something in her head, because then she added, with a wicked giggle, 'Not physically anyway.'

Which didn't do much for Millie's nerves.

Tanith opened the door.

*****

Tanith showed Millie to an old wickerwork armchair that creaked loudly whenever she moved, then bustled around lighting beeswax candles and a small cone of bitter-smelling incense before disappearing behind a model theatre with an ornate proscenium arch and red velvet curtains.

Millie had been in this room several times before, and couldn't remember seeing the theatre, yet now it seemed to be taking up half the room. On the other hand, she couldn't see any dolls either, which ought to have been a relief, but instead their absence made her nervous. At least when you could *see* the dolls, you knew where they were and what they were up to.

She shook her head, smiling to herself. They were dolls! What could they possibly be up to, other than sitting around, being inanimate and doll-like?

The incense was beginning to make her head spin, but just as she was debating whether to ask Tanith if she could go to bed after all, her ears picked up a sudden skittering noise. It was coming from behind the red velvet, which undulated slightly in a current of air she could see but not feel. Her arms erupted into goose pimples, and not from cold. Whatever this was, she wasn't sure she wanted to go through with it.

'Tanith?' she said in a small voice.

No answer. Instead, the curtains twitched, once, twice, before being drawn back in a series of herky-jerky movements, each lurch accompanied by a loud squeaking, like the sound of trolley wheels that hadn't been sufficiently oiled.

Millie found herself gazing at a painted set representing a rural landscape. A pair of conjoined cottages stood at the bottom of a gentle valley.

The landscape was two dimensional, and yet wasn't. It was made up of flat cut-outs, like theatre scenery, shaped to resemble trees or low hills in different sizes, set one behind the other to give the illusion of perspective and drawing the eye back a long, long way to a distant horizon. Indeed, the cut-outs stretched back so far Millie wondered how they could still be contained within the room, which she hadn't realised was such a large one. Probably a clever optical illusion, she decided.

Then the dolls entered. At first, Millie had to stifle a nervous giggle, because although they looked every bit as creepy as she remembered, they were all different sizes and entirely the wrong scale, both for the setting and for each other.

The largest was a baby doll that loomed like Godzilla not just over the other dolls, but over the cottages too. The smallest was a china doll with a cracked face that gave it the air of a scarred gangster, a likeness made even more disturbing by its bright blue eyes and tiny white teeth just visible behind plump rosebud lips. There was another doll with matted auburn hair in plaits, and an arm missing, and an orange-skinned mannikin whose blurry, indistinct features made it look as though it had been left too close to a fire and had half-melted.

The dolls moved like the curtain, in a series of jerky movements accompanied by that same squeaky sound, with the skittering noise in the background. If

Millie thought too hard about it (and she didn't like to think too hard) the skittering reminded her of the pattering of tiny clawed paws, scampering up and down. Was the house infested by mice? She pushed that thought firmly aside, and instead tired to concentrate on working out how Tanith was making the dolls move. She couldn't see any strings. Maybe they had rods fixed to their backs? But there were so many of them!

And then one of the dolls passed in front of the other, something she didn't think would be possible if they were attached to rods. Unless... Unless Tanith was *under* the theatre, manipulating the rods from there. But in that case, how was she managing to make all the dolls move at once, as they were doing now, shifting positions and swapping places? Was there someone else in the room, helping her?

And now the dolls were speaking as well. Millie couldn't actually see their mouths moving, but she didn't just know the voices were coming from the dolls, she knew exactly which doll was speaking at any given time.

'This is the most promising so far,' said the baby doll, peering into the middle distance. 'Woodland to the west, marshes to the south, hills to the north and east. What do you think, Tanith? Can we protect it?'

Millie jumped, not just at the sound of Tanith's name, but because the doll's voice had been familiar - not a doll's voice at all. She'd heard that doll's voice before, and recently...

Mrs. Crumley! The baby doll had Mrs. Crumley's voice! It had to be a trick - some sort of miniature loudspeaker inside the head, perhaps - but if so, it was a pretty clever one.

The doll with the cracked face answered, waving its arms as though to illustrate its words. 'Rill to the south, brook to the west, assorted rivulets honeycombing the hills to the north. We should be able to link them up without too much trouble.'

Millie felt her mouth open in surprise. This doll had Tanith's voice.

'The weakest spot is the east. According to the charts, there was a stream there once, but now it's just a ditch.'

'Can we flood it?' Another familiar-sounding voice, but this one Millie couldn't identify.

'Not permanently,' said the Tanith-doll, 'but we might be able to find some way of redirecting part of the rill in an emergency.'

'You think it'll come to that?'

'It will always come to that. It's not perfect, but it'll do. It'll have to do. We don't have time on our side. The child will be with us in five days, and we have to be ready for it.'

'Just the one?'

'I'm afraid so.' The Tanith-doll looked downcast. 'We'll be giving up enough dibs as it is.'

'That doesn't seem fair,' said the Crumley-doll.

'It isn't fair. But if we do our jobs properly, she won't feel as though she has the better deal. And she'll be a target, don't forget.'

The orange doll with the melted features chipped in, in an unexpectedly deep voice. A man's voice. 'An entire village, in less than a week! Are you mad? It'll kill us.'

Dr. Scott, thought Millie.

'We can do it,' said the Tanith-doll. 'We *have* to do it.'

'What shall we call it?' asked the Crumley-doll.

'Mudville,' said a jointed wooden doll with pink-painted cheeks and another familiar-sounding voice she couldn't quite place.

'Too American,' said a doll in an Alpine peasant costume. 'How about something basic, like Hamlet?'

'Too Shakespearean!' said the jointed wooden doll.

'Little Dripping,' said a doll in a crinoline. It spoke with a man's voice. Again, Millie had the feeling she'd heard the voice before.

'Too interesting!' said Tanith. 'We want a name that people will forget within minutes of hearing it.'

'Woods over there, brambles over here,' said the doll with Dr. Scott's voice. 'How about Bramblewood?'

'Bramblewood?' said the Tanith-doll. 'That's boring. That'll do nicely.'

'Bramblewood it is,' said the Crumley-doll.

'I've forgotten it already,' said the doll in the crinoline.

Millie blinked. She was tired, so perhaps she kept her eyes closed a few beats longer than she'd intended.

But it was when she opened them again that things got *really* weird.

Chapter 11
The Stones

Even before she opened her eyes, she could smell grass, earth and clean air. Not so very different from Bramblewood's usual aromatic repertoire, then, but somehow cooler and fresher, and without even the faint undertone of coconut and vanilla that seemed to be the signature perfume of Tanith's house.

The miniature theatre was gone. Millie could feel the warmth of the sun on her face. There was a distant ticking of insects and rustle of leaves. A light breeze ruffled her hair. She looked up and saw a small flock of starlings overhead. The sky wasn't all blue, but the clouds were fluffy and unthreatening.

It was a summer's day, and she was no longer in Tanith's guest room. She was outside, standing in the middle of an overgrown field, up to her waist in weeds.

Or was she? Millie looked down at herself. Or rather, she didn't; she couldn't look at herself because she was no longer there, any more than the miniature theatre, which seemed to have vanished into thin air, and Tanith's guest room along with it. Millie pinched her own arm, and felt the pinch, but could no longer see her arm. She was invisible!

The thought made her giddy, and for a few seconds she thought she could smell the incense that Tanith had lit in the guest room after all. But then the giddiness passed, and the only scents in her nostrils were of the grass and the earth and the brambles and the fresh country air, tainted by not a whiff of traffic or cigarette or body odour, nor even by the slightly muddy, musky smells of Bramblewood as she knew it.

She recognised one of the two cottages standing in the middle of an overgrown patch of land as her own house. Parked in the front were two expensive-looking cars, a red motorbike, and three rickety pushbikes. The house next door was Tanith's, only now there was a FOR SALE sign in one of its windows. Both houses looked shabbier than usual, the window frames flaking and dowdy, in need of a good lick of paint.

But the normally tidy garden, tended so diligently by the man she'd always assumed was her father, was out of control. She couldn't actually tell where the garden ended, if indeed it did end - it seemed to ramble away from the house and shoot off in all directions, and there was no gate, just a thicket of brambles, a field of waist-high weeds, and a half-hearted wire fence that couldn't keep anything out if it tried. And, further away, a couple of broken-down old sheds she couldn't remember ever having noticed before.

Yet to the north, Millie could see the familiar outline of Betts, Hunter's and Peggs, the hills everyone in the village knew as The Silent Three. Cutter's Peak was standing out as usual from the hills to the east, with The Snout and Hangman Hill between them. This was Bramblewood all right. But in front of her house, where the village should have been, there was nothing. No pond, no village green, no Bramblewood Arms, no St. Leonard's church, no hairdresser's. Not a single house or garage or car, apart from the two in front of the decrepit cottage. No Noose, not even a proper road - nothing but faint tracks which looked as though they would turn to mud at the first hint of rain.

The village had gone.

But not the villagers.

There were about a dozen of them gathered here. She'd never seen these people before, yet their faces were oddly familiar. It was as though she'd known them in another life. Or maybe they were related to someone she knew.

And then it hit her - she *did* know these people. There was Tanith, and there were Mrs. Crumley, Dr. Scott and Torin Figgs, and over there Drusilla and Ezekiel Metford from the pub, Esther Haze and her son Patrick, Gwen and Freddy Curd, Dina and Perry Vaughan, Quentin Withers who ran the ironmongers, and Cornelia Much from the teashop that Millie hardly ever went into because it was so boring and stank of bleach...

A lot of villagers were gathered here, in fact, but they all looked different. They were younger. Thinner and prettier and younger. Much younger. It was hard to tell by how much, exactly, but it had to be at least twenty years. Maybe thirty, or forty. Maybe more. And they were dressed in nothing like their usual style. These clothes were brighter. No whiskery tweed, rumpled raincoat or drab twill. Now there was denim and velvet and lace and suede and chiffon and jewellery. A lot of jewellery, perhaps more than was strictly tasteful.

Tanith looked not much older than Millie herself; she was dressed in tight black jeans and a silk shirt patterned with a recurring skull motif, and Patrick Haze was no longer a middle-aged mummy's boy in a cardigan but barely out of his teens, and Harold Jones was in a garish Hawaiian shirt, with his hair in a ponytail, and his cousin Mick Spicer was wearing... no it couldn't be true, she had to be dreaming... *leather trousers.*

The villagers were all there, and all of them were younger. Presumably they'd arrived in the cluster of cars and vans Millie could now see parked at the end of Ferret Lane... Except that Ferret Lane wasn't there either.

Nor was the village.

Either Tanith had hypnotised her, or she was hallucinating, or...

Understanding came to Millie in an almost blinding flash, and though the insight seemed preposterous, she embraced it, because it was the only thing that made any kind of sense. This wasn't all in her head. The village didn't exist, because the village had yet to be built. The villagers were looking younger because they *were* younger.

Somehow she had travelled back through time, to an era in the distant past.

Wondering what youthful versions of Aurelia and Marcus Greenwood might look like, she scanned the small crowd in front of her. She couldn't see anyone who even faintly resembled the people she'd thought were her parents, but there wasn't time to be disappointed, because something was happening. Tanith was taking charge; she was acting as though she already had a plan half-worked out in her head. The others straggled after her in an untidy bunch as she set off in a huge circle, starting at the pair of cottages.

'Who lives here?'

Torin Figgs, no longer bald and stooped and liver-spotted, but young and fit, with a head of long and lustrous hair, had been put in charge of the paperwork. 'Only one of these is occupied,' he said, shuffling through his documents. 'Edward and Louise Hook. Middle-aged professional couple with an eighteen-year-old son, Tarquin, wants to be a musician. Moved here from London a couple of years ago, sank all their savings into this place, intending to fix it up. They have a flat in town as well. But he's been downsized, she's working from home, things are tough for them. Son's a bit of a slacker. They're mortgaged to the hilt.'

'Good,' said Tanith. 'Tell them we'll pay off their mortgage, and then give them deeds to that house we saw on the other side of Hangman Hill. It's bigger, prettier and in better repair. I don't think Tarquin will take much persuading to move back to London; help him find a flatshare, preferably with other would-be musicians. Then put a glyph on them. Make them forget they ever lived here, and make them steer clear of this valley for, oh, the next thirty years. No, let's be on the safe side, it'll only be a few dibs extra, *fifty* years. And of course make them forget they ever saw us. And for heaven's sake make sure the other cottage is taken off the estate agent's books. We don't want house hunters turning up at an awkward moment. You don't even need to waste dibs on that.'

Dina Vaughan, who instead of her usual wispy grey bun had long and wavy red hair and was wearing a top decorated with a Japanese kitty-kat appliqué, jotted something down in a notebook. 'Consider it done.'

Tanith turned her back on the cottages. 'All this,' she waved her arms, 'will be the village green. We can dress up a Preemo as a lamppost, put that there... Maybe a pond over here.'

'How about some sifflers on the pond?' suggested Freddy Curd, who was dressed in low-rise jeans that exposed an inch of underpant waistband.

'Good idea,' said Tanith. 'And over there...' She waved her arms again. 'I suggest we put the church over there, as far away from the child as possible. I don't want Pardew hovering over her any more than is necessary.'

'Shouldn't we wait till he gets here before we start on the church?' asked Esther Haze. 'He'll probably want a say in the design.'

'We don't even need to ask,' said Ezekiel Metford. 'We know what he wants. Gothic. The grimmer the better.'

'If he wants a say in the design, let him cough up some of his own dibs,' said Dina. 'I don't mind doing it for the child, but I'm not giving him any of mine.'

Some of the villagers looked uncomfortable. Then Dina added what they had all been thinking. 'Do we really have to have him on board?'

'He's such a party-pooper,' said Ezekiel. 'Last time we collaborated he got carried away and tried to get *us* shut down. Takes his calling far too seriously. You know he'd have us all burnt at the stake if he could. He's more Witchfinder General than C of E.'

'Sorry guys, we need him,' said Dr. Scott. (But was he really a doctor? Millie wasn't sure any more. With the years pruned away from him, he looked barely old enough to shave, let alone to have been through medical school.) 'Hunters are hard to come by these days. We need his knowledge and expertise.'

Millie was so distracted by Dr. Scott's youthful looks that she almost missed what he said. But not quite.

Hunters are hard to come by? *Hunters?* In red coats, on horseback? Millie couldn't remember ever having seen a hunt anywhere near Bramblewood, though she wasn't sorry about that, because she liked foxes.

'Kevin's right,' said Tanith. (Dr. Scott's name was Kevin? The revelations were coming thick and fast.) 'We need him more than he needs us. I know he can be a pain, but we'll just have to put up with it.'

The group fragmented into smaller factions which started chattering among themselves, and Millie found it hard to pick up the thread till Drusilla Metford, who instead of her usual utilitarian calf-length smock was wearing rather a nice paisley-patterned mini-skirt that showed off unexpectedly long and well-toned legs, raised her voice to cut through the babble.

'So who's going to mow this lawn?'

'Hardly a lawn,' said Cornelia Much. 'More like a jungle. That'll be at least twenty dibs before we can even get started.'

'I believe this is your speciality, Darius,' said Mrs. Crumley. 'Do you need help?'

'No problem,' said Darius Chattox, who was dressed in a scruffy biker's jacket, nothing like his usual tweed, and cool-looking wire-rimmed spectacles instead of the familiar horn rims. He had a nice head of hair too, thought Millie, a long way from the usual bald patch.

'Now?'

'Might as well,' said Dr. Scott. 'Time is of the essence.'

Darius took his jacket off, folded it, placed it on the ground and patted it fondly, like someone taking leave of a beloved pet. The others fell silent and watched as he waded out into the long grass until he was standing, Millie calculated, round about where she was used to seeing the lamppost.

'Good luck,' someone called. A few of the others echoed the sentiment.

'Thank you,' said Darius, a little sadly. He closed his eyes and placed his forefingers on his eyelids.

For a while, nothing happened.

'Ought we to chip in?' Drusilla Metford asked in a stage whisper.

'Let him do it his way,' said Dr. Scott.

Even from where she was standing, Millie could see the veins in Darius Chattox's temples throbbing. They throbbed once, twice, and his nose began to bleed, but just as she began to worry that he was having a stroke, or maybe a heart attack, she saw the ground around them ripple.

And not just around them, she saw now - all the land for several hundred yards in every direction was rippling as though it wasn't earth but a massive lake with a riptide moving across the surface. It rippled, and shimmered, and even flickered a little. And when all the rippling and shimmering and bubbling had stopped, all the brambles and the weeds and the broken-down sheds and everything else had gone.

Darius Chattox sank to his knees, blood trickling from his nose. He no longer looked like the chipper young chap of only a few moments earlier, but pale and exhausted. Even his hair looked thinner. The other villagers stared at him in horror, but eventually Jessica Vespers pulled herself together and hurried over to offer him a handkerchief to staunch his nosebleed. Millie marvelled at the speed at which she covered the ground - the old Miss Vespers she knew could barely move three yards without the help of a Zimmer Frame.

'Are you OK, Darius?' called Tanith. There was a wobble in her voice.

Darius mumbled something incoherent, but managed to give a thumbs-up sign.

Janet Procter, whom Millie knew as the mumsy hairdresser who ran Brenda's Beauty Salon (and whose hair, normally crimped into an unforgiving mauve-rinsed perm, now tumbled over her shoulders in a buttery blonde curtain) planted herself in front of Tanith and began to gesticulate wildly. Tanith looked upset. Millie edged closer to try and hear what they were saying.

'You can walk away at any time,' said Tanith, 'if you want to stay forever young and beautiful... like *them*. No one is forcing you to give up your dibs.'

'I want to help,' said Janet. 'I really do, but... just *look* at Darius! Is that how we're all going to end up?'

'We're not doing this for fun,' said Tanith. 'You know perfectly well that if Maison Pim gets its hands on the child none of our lives will be worth living. Being young and beautiful won't save you, Janet. It won't save any of us. Anyway, it's only a few wrinkles. You're as young as you feel.'

She didn't sound convinced, but Janet nodded slowly. 'You're right, I'm sorry. It's just...'

Tanith patted her on the shoulder. 'I know. It's tough. I wish there were more of us left to share the load. I wish there were some other way. But there isn't.'

*****

The land had been cleared, and now it was time to plan the layout.

The villagers split into three groups, each taking a large doctor's bag in battered brown leather. One group set off towards the south, another headed east, but Millie chose to stay behind with Tanith, Janet, Dr. Scott, Mrs. Crumley (whose first name, Millie learned, was Amelia) and the Metfords. She tagged along, eavesdropping, as they set off in a wide circle, sometimes stopping to jot down notes or measurements, or pausing to disagree. There were a lot of disagreements.

'Remember,' said Tanith. 'Nothing too pretty or picturesque. We want this to be the sort of place no one will ever want to visit.'

So it was that Millie witnessed the birth of Bramblewood, a village that - up until that sunny day in September - hadn't existed. It didn't appear on any map, and if Tanith and the others had anything to do with it, never would. Visitors were to be discouraged, it seemed.

Once they'd decided on the placement of the buildings, Ezekiel Metford opened the doctor's bag and each of the villagers withdrew fistfuls of small stones, which they placed carefully, though not without a great deal of discussion and bickering about which stone should go where, in the newly shortened grass, marking walls and doors and gardens and garages. They mapped out what Millie knew would be the Vaughans' house, then the cottage shared by Harold Jones and Mick Spicer, then walked a short way down what would one day be known as Bramblewood Road to lay the foundations of Bethany Brod's studio and then, opposite that, Dr. Scott's house with its adjoining surgery and office.

When they'd finished deciding on the outline of Mrs. Crumley's shop, Millie loitered behind, letting the group walk on towards the site of Janet's hairdressing salon. She crouched down to examine the markers more closely. The stones varied - some were round and flat; others had unexpectedly sharp angles, or odd little bumps. But they all seemed to be fashioned out of a waxy black substance shot through with green or red or purple, depending on which angle you were looking from. They reminded Millie of the shifting colours of the pearl.

She checked to make sure no one was watching - she might have been invisible, but she was aware the stones weren't - and prodded one, half-expecting her finger to pass right through it. But to her surprise, she could feel it with her fingertip. Without really thinking, she picked it up and weighed it in her palm. It was unexpectedly heavy, and when the light caught it at a certain angle she could see fine symbols etched into the surface. They were not letters of the Roman alphabet, nor were they - as far as she knew - Greek or Russian. If anything, they reminded her of the runes from J. R. R. Tolkien's books, the ones that Julia Evans and Andrew Quigley were always writing.

'Shouldn't we put the Pendleburys here?' Tanith was asking.

'Better post them on the far side of the cottage,' said Drusilla. 'You'll be monitoring the other side, and Gwen and Freddy can watch your back...'

'Yes, I agree,' said Dr. Scott (Millie found it impossible to think of him as Kevin). 'But don't forget to put some distance between the Curds and Hilary and

Violet. You know how dogs can set them off, and we need to avoid false alarms wherever possible.'

Millie was listening to all this with mild bemusement (the idea of the doddery old Pendlebury sisters being 'set off' in any way struck her as almost outlandish) while idly tracing the runes on the waxy black stone with her finger, when suddenly she felt something budge and looked down. A tiny hole had opened up in the stone's surface, and an equally tiny tube had popped out as though it had been spring-loaded. She coaxed the tube all the way out with the tips of her fingernails, and found it was a miniature coil of parchment, or some other similar material, and that there was something printed on the inner surface...

Just as she was on the point of unrolling the coil, she heard a yelp and looked up. Mrs. Crumley was staring straight at her. Or rather, staring at the black stone, which - seemingly of its own accord, from Mrs. Crumley's point of view - was hovering some feet above the ground. Millie drew her breath in sharply and dropped the stone, then tried to kick it back to where she'd found it, before remembering she was still holding the tiny roll of parchment, which she stuffed into her invisible pocket. To her relief, as soon as the parchment was in the pocket, it became invisible too.

'I do hope that's not a Beagle,' said Mrs. Crumley.

Everyone turned to follow her gaze. Millie froze. A beagle? Where? She hadn't seen any dogs, but with everything that was happening she wouldn't have been surprised to see some kind of boisterous hound materialising out of the air right in front of her.

'What did you see?' asked Ezekiel, taking a few steps forward. He seemed to be sniffing the air, a bit like a dog himself, Millie thought. She wondered if he could smell her presence. But after a few heart-stopping moments, he said, 'It's OK. Definitely not a Beagle. A bird, maybe?'

'They have birds too,' said Mrs. Crumley. 'Watch out for crows.'

'I can't see anything,' said Janet, staring straight at Millie but clearly not able to *see* her.

'It's nothing,' said Tanith. 'I probably misplaced one of my stones and it got a little frisky, that's all. Come on, we've still got a lot of work to do...'

She spread her arms to shepherd the group towards the spot destined to play host to Brenda's Beauty Salon. But just before turning away she looked back at Millie, just for a second, and winked.

Millie gasped, but Tanith had already moved on. Could Tanith see her? Millie reminded herself that her aunt was the reason she was here, witnessing the birth of Bramblewood, so of course she would be aware of Millie's presence.

On the other hand, this was young Tanith, not the middle-aged woman who lived next door and who was now Millie's legal guardian. Did young and old Tanith share some sort of mental connection? But how could they even exist at the same time? Millie's head began to ache at the possibilities, so she stopped trying to think about it.

All the same, she was careful not to touch anything else as she shadowed the small group of villagers around the wide looping route they would soon be calling The Noose.

*****

Watching them place the stones on the sites of the buildings she knew so well was so absorbing that Millie barely noticed the hours passing. At last, as the low sun was casting a warm glow over the trees behind her house, all three groups of villagers finished their stone-laying and gathered in the space allocated for the village green.

'Well, that's the easy part,' said Harold.

'I'm not looking forward to this,' said Gwen Curd. She turned to her husband, Freddy, of the underpants waistband. 'Will you still love me when I'm old and grey?'

He grasped her hands and smiled. 'Always, my darling.' She smiled back, and they nuzzled each other affectionately.

'Get a room!' yelled Quentin.

Everyone laughed, but to Millie's ears the laughter sounded slightly hysterical, as though the villagers were so intent on putting on a show of good spirits they had inadvertently allowed a note of desperation to creep in through the back door.

'Can't we put it off till tomorrow?' asked Amelia Crumley.

'Don't know about you,' said Perry Vaughan, 'but I'd rather get it over and done with. And anyway, I fancy sleeping in a proper bed, for once. These last few weeks have been hell on my back.'

'I agree,' said Darius, who had perked up a little since the last time Millie had seen him, though he still looked as though he'd just stumbled in from a twenty-mile hike across rough terrain. 'I'm fed up with sleeping in the car.'

'Let's go for it then,' said Tanith. 'You all know what to do? We don't want to waste dibs on silly disagreements at the manifestation stage.'

'I just hope this kid is grateful,' said Torin.

Dr. Scott said, 'If we do our job properly, she'll never even know.'

'And don't forget,' said Tanith. 'Nothing picturesque. I know it's hard, but please resist the temptation to add ivy, or honeysuckle. The last thing we need is coachloads of tourists swarming around taking holiday snaps. And no interesting bookshops either. This place has to be so dull that no one will ever want to stop here, not even for a cup of tea. The pub has to appear so unwelcoming that any thirsty travellers who happen across it will take one look and drive on. The church has to be so grim that no passing couple will decide it will be the perfect place for them to get married. In fact, be careful the green doesn't look too green. We don't want picnickers.'

I might have known it, Millie whispered to herself. *They made Bramblewood boring on purpose!*

Chapter 12
Bramblewood

Millie had no idea what was going to happen next, but assumed it would have something to do with the waxy black stones that had been laid out in a circular configuration in the space Darius Chattox had cleared without the help of a single gardening tool, apparently using nothing more than the power of his mind. She still found it hard to believe what she had just seen.

The villagers spread out until they were forming a large ring, each facing outward, away from each other and towards the stones.

And then they began to conjure Bramblewood out of the earth.

Some of them closed their eyes. Some, but not all, planted their feet apart or raised their arms or tipped their heads back, as though to drink in the dying remnants of daylight, but there didn't appear to be any one regulated approach - each had their own individual technique.

Millie backed into the doorway of what would be Tanith's cottage; no one had placed any stones there, so she surmised it would be as safe a vantage point as any.

To begin with, there wasn't much to see. She realised afterwards they'd been laying foundations beneath the surface, for even villages built by supernatural means need solid underpinnings, so they don't collapse in the first storm. But then the ground began to ripple, as it had rippled when Darius had cleared it of unwanted vegetation. Except now the rippling came in a series of criss-cross waves that spread every which way, like the surface of an ocean ruffled by contradictory breezes, shimmering in the light of the late afternoon.

And then the black stones began to wobble and bob, as if they were alive. At first, Millie thought it was a small earth tremor making them move, though the ground beneath her feet couldn't have felt any more solid and dependable. But to the east, the earth itself began to bubble and shift and arrange itself into a spiky outline, which grew higher and wider and darker until Millie finally recognised what she was seeing: the spire of St. Leonard's church. Still smoky and insubstantial, but, while she watched, it gained in solidity and bulk as it took on the familiar witch's hat shape.

The church was obviously going to be bigger than all the other buildings; Tanith, Darius and Dina Vaughan were having to combine forces. Millie saw them shaping the apse and chancel before they began to install pillars on either side of the nave. The air itself seemed to be shimmering as the pillars thrust upward, like stone trees in a forest. It was all quite spectacular, but Millie spotted something that made her uneasy; a streak of grey in Tanith's hair she could have sworn hadn't been there a few moments earlier. And it wasn't just Tanith's hair that was turning grey - Dina had acquired more than a few silvery highlights, while Darius's formerly healthy mane was thinning so rapidly that shiny patches of pink scalp were now visible.

The change coming over them was frightening, but the construction of the church, piece by piece, was so compelling that Millie found it hard to tear her eyes away and pay attention to what was going on in the rest of the village. When finally she did, she let out a gasp. Bramblewood was taking shape in front of her. To the left of the church, Drusilla and Ezekiel were squeezing each other's hands tightly as they raised the walls of the building that would presently be known as the Bramblewood Arms. They were sketching the outline like a drawing, and then painstakingly filling it in with colour and form. It looked like extremely hard work, requiring a concentration that was making their shoulders tense. From where she was standing she couldn't see their faces, but their hair, too, looked thinner.

Similar scenes were taking place all around the patch of scrub that would soon be known as the village green. To the left of the Metfords, Janet was busily embedding what looked like a series of washbasins into one side of Brenda's Beauty Parlour, putting her hands on her hips and twisting this way and that, as though deciding what kind of taps to install.

Amelia Crumley seemed to be having trouble with one side of her post-office and corner shop; she kept repeating the same gesture, her brusque movements betraying a mounting irritation. Millie's heart skipped a beat as she realised the wall causing so much grief was the exact spot where she had picked up the stone. Had she put it back in the wrong place? Well, she couldn't do anything about it now, and besides there was too much happening elsewhere.

Nearby, Dr. Scott was preoccupied with the ground floor of his house and surgery, while across the road Bethany was knotting her brows over a stubborn bay window. And even now, to Millie's immediate left, Harold and Mick seemed to be having a last-minute disagreement about the size of their kitchen. To her right, Esther Haze was helping Gwen and Freddy Curd on the construction of two buildings, one the house where the Pendlebury sisters were to be installed (Millie hadn't seen either Hilary and Violet, and surmised - correctly, as it turned out - their presence hadn't been required because they just weren't very good at building houses, though they did possess other talents that might one day come in useful) and then, a little further back, the house and adjoining veterinary consultation room.

Michelle Gowery was shuffling on the spot like a tap dancer as she added a porch to her house, and Cornelia Much's face was twitching as she conjured the black and white tiles on the floor of her tearoom. Torin Figgs was flapping his arms uncontrollably, like a bird caught in a fence, though it seemed to be doing the trick - he'd got as far as adding a staircase to his house. Martha Putnam had left most of the construction of Bramble Farm to her husband Harvey, and was applying herself to the ground floor of the ironmonger's, while Quentin was concentrating on his metalworking shop. Patrick Haze, who seemed to have boundless energy, was helping Jessica with her bungalow while simultaneously working on the house he would be soon sharing with his mother.

Meanwhile the church was sprouting in all directions, like a dark and wayward plant. Darius, exhausted by the effort, had sunk to his knees, but

Tanith and Dina continued to add columns, an aisle, an altar and the beginnings of some stained glass windows, too murky and commonplace to draw the attention of any stray arts and crafts enthusiasts who might take a wrong turning off the main road.

The village was taking shape, though it was still insubstantial, not quite all there, as though a stiff breeze might yet blow it away. But little by little, from the ground up, the buildings were becoming more solid. Walls and staircases were added to floors, then doors and windows and, finally, roofs - some tiled, others thatched. But the thatching wasn't picturesque, of course; it looked grimy and infested.

Millie was fascinated. If this were all a dream (and she still wasn't sure that it wasn't) then it was a peculiarly intricate one. But her uneasiness was growing as well. Ezekiel Metford, Gwen Curd and Perry Vaughan all had nosebleeds. Quentin Withers was bleeding from his ears, and Cornelia Much was holding her face between her hands as though she feared it might detach itself and fly away. Darius wasn't the only one whose energies were being drained. The villagers themselves were shrinking, becoming more stooped and desiccated before Millie's anxious gaze. Their hands were curling into claws, spattered with fresh liver spots. Rivulets of grey were running through their hair; Torin Figgs's scalp was gleaming.

They were ageing decades before Millie's eyes.

What they're doing here is costing them their youth, she realised. And there was no reclaiming it; what was done was done, and there would be no going back. There had been a reason everyone in Bramblewood - everyone except Millie, that is - had been so aged and decrepit, and now here it was, right in front of her. She felt a stab of guilt, remembering how often she had moaned to Paula about being stuck in a village full of creaky old pensioners.

But the fruit of their efforts was there for everyone to see. The Bramblewood Millie knew wasn't complete - there were roofs and windows missing, and as yet no gardens, nor (from what she could see) furniture. It was Bramblewood in embryo, but definitely Bramblewood. And though it had been expressly designed to be the most boring village in England, she was now starting to find it fascinating. The village had secrets. More than that, the village itself *was* a secret, that much was becoming clear.

But the villagers were falling like flies. First Harold keeled over, then Jessica's legs gave way, then Freddy Curd bent double, clutching his stomach. Tanith, who seemed to be bearing up better than most, paused in the middle of inserting some gloomy stained glass into a window and glanced anxiously at the others.

'We should take a break,' she said. 'That'll do for today.'

'What about the school?' asked Dr. Scott.

There was a chorus of groans.

'The school can wait,' said Tanith. 'We have a few years to sort that out, and obviously we'll need to involve Gwen and the nine families. Besides, I think we're all just about ready to drop.'

'Hold on,' said Perry Vaughan, wiping his nose. 'Just let me...' He performed an elaborate movement with his blood-streaked left hand. 'There!'

More blood came out of his nose, but Dina clapped her hands with delight. 'A bed! You're so clever, darling. Let me add a duvet and pillows.' Her movements mimicked those of her husband. Millie couldn't *see* any changes, but she somehow sensed that the Vaughans' house, on the other side of Tanith's cottage, now contained an insanely comfortable double bed.

'Good idea,' said Tanith, looking shattered. She turned in Millie's direction and did something with her own left hand. Millie tried to get out of the way before realising that Tanith's aim was not directed at her, but at the upper floor of her house.

'I'm so wiped out I could fall asleep on a concrete slab,' said Drusilla, but all around the circle, stricken villagers began to summon what was left of their strength to create comfortable sleeping arrangements.

'Wait,' said Dr. Scott. 'We can't flake out all together like this. We'll be leaving ourselves wide open. It would be ironic if the Beagles caught up with us just as we're creating our safe haven. We need to set up a guardian, maybe two.'

'He's right,' said Amelia Crumley. 'Does anyone still have enough energy to stay up and keep watch? We can take it in turns. But someone needs to do the first shift, which will be hard.'

'I've got a better idea,' said Tanith. 'How are you feeling, Bethany?'

Bethany Brod sighed. 'Could be worse. You're thinking we bring out the Greenwoods tonight?'

Millie's ears pricked up. Greenwoods? Did that mean Aurelia and Marcus were coming?

'We can all chip in,' said Clive Crisp, whom Millie didn't know very well. She sometimes saw him in church, but he lived with his wife Bernadette in the big house just outside the village. She turned now and craned her neck and glimpsed its half-finished roof in the distance, against the darkening backdrop of trees that marked the edge of the forest.

Bethany shook her head wearily. 'Better if I fly solo. We don't want to get our wires crossed. The glyph needs to be as pure as possible for it to endure, and if more than one of us works on it there are bound to be glitches down the line.'

'As you wish,' said Clive, sounding a little miffed.

'Bethany's the expert,' said Dr. Scott. 'She's done this before, many times. She won't need as many dibs as the rest of us.'

Bethany made a face. 'It'll take a chunk out of my dib count, all the same. But yeah, better if you leave it to me.'

The others gathered round to watch. Millie hadn't noticed Patrick break away from the group, but now he came haring back from the parked cars, carrying a carpetbag, more voluminous than the doctors' bags that had contained the stones. He set it down next to Bethany, who extracted four fat red candles, placed them in a large square configuration, round about where the duck pond would be. She lit each candle with a different match. They were strange matches, more like tapers than matches, in fact, and each flared up with a greenish flame that turned orange as Bethany applied it to the wick of a candle.

By now it was dark, but the candles lit the scene with an eerie glow. Bethany swept her hair back into a loose ponytail so it wouldn't fall over her face, and knelt down on the ground between two of the candles, plunging her arms into the earth. Then she began to chant words in a foreign language that Millie didn't recognise. She made an effort to memorise some of the words, so she could look them up later online, but the sounds were barely pronounceable, let alone comprehensible, and slithered away from her even as she tried to get a grip on them.

Bethany was rocking backwards and forwards, chanting all the while as she pulled handfuls of red soil out of the earth and moulded them, bit by bit, into two long shapes. The others watched, just as fascinated as Millie, as more and more handfuls were added to the shapes, until each looked like the sort of soft-edged form you might construct out of pillows and blankets to hoodwink your parents into thinking you were lying asleep in your bed, when actually you'd already climbed out of your window and set out on some nocturnal adventure. Millie had never actually done this, but she'd read stories about people who had, and more than once had fantasised about doing it herself.

At last, Bethany seemed satisfied with the shapes she had formed, and rocked back on her heels to reopen the carpet bag. This time she extracted two tiny rolls of parchment, much like the one Millie had earlier thrust into her pocket. As though threading needles, Bethany inserted the parchment into the earth, one in each pile; she seemed to picking the insertion points with care and precision.

Then she took out two bundles of cloth, carefully unravelling each bundle before laying it on top of the earthen shapes. Millie saw they were sets of clothes. On one shape Bethany laid out a man's blue suit and pale blue shirt, on the other a grey pleated skirt and white blouse with a pussycat bow, and a string of pearls.

Millie gasped. The clothes looked almost identical to the ones her parents wore. No, not *almost* identical - they *were* identical.

A dreadful worm of suspicion began to uncoil in Millie's brain, but she could only watch, hypnotised, as Bethany dipped into the bag again before hauling herself to her feet. In her hand was a jar, the contents of which she began to sprinkle in a circle around the four candles and the two recumbent shapes. It looked like some sort of crystalline powder, maybe salt, or bicarbonate of soda. As she sprinkled, she resumed her chanting, until the circle she'd made was complete. Bethany returned to the bag and this time came out with a long stick - so long that Millie couldn't fathom how it had fitted into the bag, which was big, but not *that* big. The stick - it was actually more of a staff than a stick - was the size of a slender branch from a tree. In fact it might even have been a branch, since there were leaves still attached to it.

Summoning what little remained of her energy, Bethany began to wave it, slowly, from side to side, as she walked around the circle, keeping her unblinking eyes fixed on the earthen shapes. Tendrils of hair had escaped from her ponytail, and she appeared to have shed a lot of weight in only the past ten minutes or so; her clothes were hanging off her.

Millie had never really taken much notice of Bethany Brod before, but was now starting to find her a little frightening.

Bethany's chanting grew louder and louder as she began to flick the branch towards the shapes, as though trying to shake droplets of water on to the ground.

The heaps of earth looked ominous, like burial mounds harbouring dark secrets that ought never to be dug up. There was a deep rumbling from somewhere beneath Millie's feet. She retreated into Tanith's porch as far as she could, until her back was right up against the rickety door, and noticed that even some of the villagers looked nervous. The Metfords were clutching each other, as if for comfort, and Quentin was chewing his nails.

Bethany sank to her knees and her head slumped forward. Several of the villagers started forward, as if to help, but Tanith waved them back and mouthed, 'No!', stopping them in their tracks.

With a superhuman effort, Bethany raised her head, mustered the last of her resources, and, in a hoarse whisper, completed the incantation. For that, Millie now realised, was what it was.

The tension was almost unbearable. The rumbling in the earth reached a crescendo, as though a solfatara were about to explode out of the earth, but the eruption, when it came, was from above. A flash of lightning sliced through the darkening sky and forked into two, each bolt striking one of the piles of earth and sending out showers of vicious blue sparks that made the villagers shrink back in alarm.

For a long moment, nothing happened. The gathering darkness of the night was already testing the boundaries of the candlelit circle, the deadening silence not even broken by the chirruping of insects. Everyone just stared, not daring to look away. Millie wasn't sure if she could bear the suspense.

And then she had to clamp a hand over her mouth to stop herself crying out, because the heaps of earth began to move. She watched in appalled fascination as first one, then the other shape rolled from side to side, faster and faster, as if trying to shake off invisible chains. The clothes were expanding, the empty sleeves and legs filling out. They were recognisable as crude human figures now, even if the features were still amorphous, like futurist statues carved from lumps of rock.

Bethany Brod gasped out one last incantation and fainted clean away.

Patrick glanced at Tanith, who nodded; he and Cornelia darted forward to grasp Bethany by the armpits and drag her out of the circle.

But the two piles of earth inside the circle continued to evolve. Slowly, in a process both agonisingly slow and unnaturally rapid, their bodies took shape, their limbs acquired muscle, sinew and flesh, their features sharpened into living faces...

Faces that looked exactly like Aurelia and Marcus Greenwood.

Chapter 13
Pardew

Everything Millie had believed about her life was being turned upside-down. Yes, Bramblewood was boring - but only because it had been built that way. A picturesque village would have attracted tourists, and the last things the villagers wanted were tourists sniffing around. Yes, the villagers themselves were old and decrepit - but only because they had sacrificed their youth to create the village...

How long ago had this happened? Millie concluded it had to be nearly sixteen years earlier, when she had been a baby.

Because the village was being prepared for *her*, she realised that now, like a nest being lined in readiness for the chicks. And yes, Millie's parents had been cold and unfeeling - but only because they had been inhuman robots.

Robots made of earth!

Millie felt her blood run cold as she remembered the piles of red soil spilling out of the clothes on the living-room carpet. Was that all that was left of the people who'd been looking after her for nearly sixteen years? The notion was upsetting - but somehow she wasn't nearly as upset as she felt she ought to be.

In fact she felt excited - almost happy - about it, which on top of everything else made her feel guilty as well. It was a heady cocktail of emotions, too much to digest all at once, and for the first time since she'd begun to watch these strange flashbacks into Bramblewood's history she just wanted to shut her eyes and curl up and go to sleep at the end of this extraordinary day. Everything would be all right in the morning. Her parents would be there as usual when she got up, the trip to Paris had never happened, Paula and Sam had never disappeared, and life would go on as...

Except Millie wasn't sure she *wanted* everything to go back to normal. Of course she wanted Paula and Sam to be safe, but how normal was normal anyway? What if *this* were normal, and the life she had been living up until now had been nothing but a sham, a confabulation of elements combined to make everything around her seem normal, when in fact it was anything but?

It was when Aurelia and Marcus Greenwood moved that Millie's head began to throb again. The earthen figures both sat up at exactly the same moment, clumps of soil trickling down their backs like dirty bathwater, their arms held stiffly at their sides.

Millie couldn't help herself. Despite all she had seen and heard, she still wanted to run over and hug them, even if Marcus and Aurelia had never had been the hugging type. But they'd looked after her for nearly sixteen years, hadn't they? They'd been strict, but never mean. They had performed their parental duties well enough.

If only Bethany Brod had programmed them to show a little more affection towards their 'daughter', they might have been the perfect mother and father.

But when Millie looked over at the group of villagers, she saw Bethany collapsed on the ground, with

Ezekiel Metford massaging her hands and Amelia Crumley holding a small flask to her mouth, trying to coax some of its contents between her lips. Whatever Bethany had done, it had taxed her to the limit. No one could have expected more of her.

Except me, thought Millie. Couldn't she have added just a smidgeon of human warmth? Maybe the next day, after she'd had a good night's sleep? And then she felt guilty again for even thinking that. She had no idea how Bethany's enchantment, or whatever it had been, had worked. Maybe once it was finished, that was that, and the results couldn't be modified...

'Good evening.'

Millie nearly jumped out of her skin. Marcus Greenwood had spoken, but he didn't sound anything like the father she'd grown up with. His voice was like the creak of an old door that needed its hinges oiling.

'You have called us,' said Aurelia Greenwood, sounding only slightly less croaky than her husband. 'And we came.'

'We are at your service,' said Marcus.

'Welcome,' said Tanith. 'Your duties will be to...'

But her words were interrupted as several of the villagers pricked up their ears and, suddenly alert, wrenched their attention away from the Greenwood golems, whipping their heads around to the east.

Millie looked in the same direction, and saw they'd been distracted by a sudden change in the night sky: a lightening of the eastern horizon beyond Hangman Hill. Was it dawn already? Maybe she'd been so absorbed in the creation of the village that the night had passed more rapidly than she'd realised.

Then she heard the sound. The villagers were hearing it too: a low rumbling which escalated into a dragon-like roar as the light in the east grew brighter, then dimmed before growing brighter again.

Something was approaching, at speed.

And then Millie saw the lightening in the sky wasn't a sign of dawn, but the headlights of a car on the far side of Hangman Hill, the sound of the engine hacking its way through the night like a scythe through undergrowth. And it was coming closer, the engine revving and shrieking as the motorist took the hairpin bends in the hills around Cutter's Peak like a Formula One driver.

'Beagles!' shouted Jessica. 'How did they find out so quickly?'

There was an almighty kerfuffle and the villagers began to run around like headless chickens. Someone yelled, 'We've got nothing left! We're done for!'

'Calm down,' said Dr. Scott. 'It's not Beagles.'

Tanith's mouth set in a grim line. 'It's Pardew.'

Harold laughed mirthlessly. 'I almost wish it were Beagles.'

'Oh lord,' said Cornelia. 'I expect now we'll get one of his sermons. That's all I need.'

Millie looked at the approaching headlights with a mixture of dread and curiosity. The Reverend Pardew had always been her least favourite villager. On the other hand, she was curious to see what he'd looked like nearly sixteen years ago. Would he be one of those trendy guitar-playing vicars? The thought made her giggle softly to herself.

She stopped giggling as the car screamed down what would soon be known as Ferret Lane towards the villagers, who bunched together in the middle of the green, holding their arms up to try and shield their eyes from the glare of the approaching headlights. Millie had never noticed before, but they seemed to dislike the Reverend Pardew as much as as she did, and weren't at all thrilled at the prospect of seeing him.

The vehicle finally screeched to a halt, just yards from where they were clustered, but it wasn't until the dazzling headlights blinked off that she received one of the biggest surprises of that entire day. She had never been very good at identifying the makes of cars, but this was the last thing she expected to see being driven by a grinch like Pardew: a handsome vintage sports car, low-slung and bright yellow, more the type of attention-grabbing thing a famous film star might drive than conveyance for a pious man of the cloth.

The tall, gaunt figure hopped out without even bothering to open the door, and strode towards the villagers, his long black coat flapping behind him.

'You clowns!' he shouted. 'You've left a mark on the grid I could see from a hundred miles away! You call this safe?'

'We were going to wipe it off first thing in the morning,' mumbled Freddy Curd.

Pardew wasn't mollified. His beetle brows knitted together in the mother of all disapproving frowns. 'You think they'll hold off just because you need a nap? Have you any idea what you're dealing with? This is the night! This is *their* time. What if someone other than me had spotted it?'

Millie was reeling from yet another surprise. Reverend Pardew looked exactly the same as he always did, and not one minute younger. But she didn't have time to dwell on the conundrum, because the Reverend came to a sudden halt, stretched out his long arms, turning his palms upward, and gave an almighty shrug. His shoulders heaved and he muttered something that was inaudible from where she was standing. For a moment, his figure flickered, as though it were on the verge of winking out. And then it was solid again.

'There,' he said. 'I've erased your shadow from the grid, for a few hours at least. It won't hold. And what is *this* abomination?' He stabbed a bony finger at the half-finished church.

'We were waiting for your input,' said Tanith. 'We knew you'd have special requirements...'

Pardew tossed his head scornfully and strands of his long black hair - which was oily rather than lustrous - whipped through the air. 'Never let it be said that I...'

And he stopped, and swivelled, and looked straight at Millie.

'What the... I don't believe it! You've let the rabbit loose? Even before you've finished knitting the glyphs together?'

Millie quailed. His black eyes were boring straight into her. He could *see* her.

All the villagers except Tanith looked baffled.

Then Pardew let out an angry roar. 'GIRL!'

And began to stride swiftly towards her.

Millie tried to back away, but she was already up against the door of Tanith's cottage. There was nowhere for her to go.

'GIRL!'

Pardew swept straight through the villagers, scattering them like small birds. He was coming closer, a gaunt black figure with ragged garments streaming out behind him, his face twisted with unnatural fury and his finger pointing straight at her.

'GIRL!'

Millie's heart was already in her mouth, but now it stopped altogether.

And then, at her ear, she heard Tanith speaking, her voice soft and calm and fully in control of the situation. 'Don't worry, Millie. He can't hurt you. He's not really here.'

Millie hadn't been aware that her eyes were closed, but now she opened them. The Reverend Pardew was gone, and so were the half-built village and all the hills around it. She was sitting in the wickerwork armchair in Tanith's guest room. The red velvet curtains of the model theatre were drawn back to show the stage where a higgledy-piggledy heap of dolls lay framed by a two-dimensional stage set. The scenery that earlier had been nothing more than cut-outs of hills and trees was now an intricate small-scale mock-up of Bramblewood's houses and shops propped up around a village green.

Tanith was sitting beside her, stroking her hand.

'Was that a dream?' asked Millie.

'No, you were awake,' said Tanith. 'I just gave you a glimpse into the past. A flashback, if you like. You know, like in a movie. It only lasted a few minutes, though it probably seemed to you like hours.'

Millie yawned. She felt as exhausted as if she herself had just built an entire village from scratch. 'What time is it?'

'Past your bedtime, I think.'

'Was that how it happened?'

'Yes. In this version, anyway. These memories are mine, which is why I seemed to be doing most of the talking. But I'm sure the memories of someone like Michelle Gowery, say, would be different. She saw other things, had a completely different experience.'

'Like alternative universes?' asked Millie, yawning again.

'In a manner of speaking,' said Tanith. 'But this is the only version that matters, for now.'

Millie had a thousand questions she was dying to ask, but it had been a long and unnaturally eventful day. Thoughts were buzzing around her head like bluebottles, resisting her every attempt to pin them down or swat them away, but her eyelids were heavy and determined to close, no matter how hard she tried to keep them open.

Tanith looked apologetic. 'Perhaps I should have left all that for tomorrow, but it'll probably be good for you to sleep on it. It's a lot to take in, I know. We'll talk about it over breakfast.'

'Do I have to sleep in here?'

'With all these creepy dolls? Gracious, no. They wouldn't let you get any sleep at all. I've made up the bed in the room at the back.'

Millie was thankful. The small room at the back contained little more than a single bed, a chair and a table, but it was mercifully doll-free. Millie changed into a pair of paisley-patterned pyjamas Tanith had left on the counterpane; they were too big for her, but she didn't care. She was so tired she left her own clothes in a heap on the floor. She simply couldn't summon the energy to fold them neatly.

I'll do that in the morning, she vowed.

No sooner had her head made contact with the pillow then she slipped into a deep and dreamless sleep.

Chapter 14
An Inferior Armagnac

Sometimes Dupontel wondered why he was on the side of the bad guys. Because they were very, very bad, no question about it. They killed without a qualm, and then covered up the murders, or arranged it so that innocent parties were blamed. They stalked and kidnapped and imprisoned and blackmailed for their own selfish ends, and generally behaved as they pleased, without fear of reprisal, because their influence stretched far and wide, even during daylight hours, though they themselves were confined to the dark.

They had centuries of experience in the art of luring politicians, police or members of the judiciary into sticky situations. Dupontel personally knew of one very important judge who had been photographed in a compromising position on a barge with two Bichons Frises and a Nazi helmet, and who afterwards had been prepared to do anything to prevent the pictures being made public. Several high-ranking ministers and a substantial cross-section of the Parisian police force were also on the payroll, as were strategically placed media barons who invariably proved useful whenever the press got wind of a scandal that needed covering up.

Maison Pim was evil, no two ways about it.

On the plus side, it offered eternal youth and limitless wealth. On the minus, Dupontel reflected as he lit yet another cigarette, the Syndicate was bloody terrifying.

He made a concentrated effort to steady his hand, which was vibrating like a washing machine in a spin cycle. It wouldn't do to show signs of nervousness in this company. When they sensed weakness, it only made them all the more ruthless. His climb to the top of the organisation had required an unremitting slog of Olympic-level toadying, and the undertaking of the sort of distasteful tasks the Syndicate considered too demeaning to contemplate, but it would take only one false move on his part to send him plummeting back down to the bottom of the pile. And those at the bottom of the pile were expendable.

Dupontel imagined that the good guys, whoever and wherever they were, would be nicer people, who wouldn't make his hand tremble at all. They would show mercy to those who made mistakes, and treat any adversaries who strayed into their orbit with understanding and compassion. A minion such as Moreau, for example, would not now be languishing in the dungeons awaiting exsanguination; he would probably be given tea and biscuits and a sympathetic pat on the shoulder, and a stern warning not to try and kidnap anyone ever again.

On the other hand, the showing of mercy was one of their principal weaknesses. This was why they were destined to lose the monumental struggle that lay ahead of them. This was why Dupontel had chosen to side with evil. This was why he was sitting here, on one of a row of hard-backed chairs set opposite the double doors made of intricately carved oak. The carvings depicted some sort of elaborate historical ritual involving what appeared to be dismemberment and disembowelling, but Dupontel didn't feel up to examining them too closely.

The doors opened and shadow spilled out.

Dupontel swallowed, hard, and stubbed out his cigarette. This was it then. Either Miss Pim would accept what even he considered to be a series of rather feeble-sounding excuses for the errors that had occurred on his watch, and give him a second chance. Or he would be stripped of his status and hauled off into the Crypt, possibly even to share a cell with Moreau, who no doubt would be only too pleased to see his erstwhile boss laid low alongside him.

Dupontel thought sadly of his beautifully furnished apartment on Avenue Wagram and his beloved white cat, Mirabelle, who had one blue eye and one green one. Would he ever see her again? He cursed inwardly for having forgotten to make arrangements for her to be fed in the event of his abrupt disappearance. But too late now.

A figure in a mauve organza ballgown materialised in the open doorway, sucking languidly on a green cigarette in a ridiculously long ivory holder.

Odile Villeneuve.

Dupontel's heart sank. She had never liked him.

'Do come in,' she purred, sounding more like a frivolous society hostess than the ancient and thoroughly evil vampire that she was. Dupontel's heart sank even further. It was when Odile was at her most frivolous that disagreeable things tended to happen.

Still, he would put on a show of confidence. If they thought he was going to grovel for mercy, they were mistaken. He was Henri Dupontel, dammit, and one day soon he would be a vampire just like them, and then they would have to treat him with the respect he deserved. He stood up, mustered his most unflappable smile, and with his head held high, sauntered past Odile into a room that was about as cheerful as a mausoleum.

'Henri,' said Miss Pim. 'So glad you could join us.'

As if he'd had any choice in the matter.

The 'salle de meeting' had clearly been designed to make visitors feel puny and powerless. Dupontel was obliged to cross a vast marble floor, six pairs of eyes drilling into him all the way, before he finally reached the big table where Miss Pim was sitting, surrounded by her most trusted lieutenants.

The lacquered surface of the table was as highly polished as a mirror, but the only person reflected there was Dupontel himself. He forced himself to meet the dispassionate gazes of the figures who cast no reflections. His internal organs shrivelled in fear as he recognised Claude Bellinger, who had been present at the laying of the foundation stone of Notre-Dame cathedral, and whose neatly trimmed goatee and charcoal grey suit gave him a Mephistophelean air.

Next to Bellinger, in flowing yellow silk, sat Melisande de Rochefort, whose plump red lips and cascading auburn curls gave her a look of youthfulness Dupontel knew was deceptive, since she had witnessed the French Revolution - had in fact played a key role in fomenting some of its bloodiest purges.

Ferdinand Martinez, clad in a Napoleonic hussar's tunic, squinted through a monocle that was wholly for show, since Martinez had 20/20 vision, and indeed had enjoyed himself enormously as a freelance sniper, picking off targets on all sides during nocturnal forays at Sevastopol, the Somme and Stalingrad.

The blue velvet jacket and carefully cultivated moustache of Pierre Duray made him look like an effete dandy, though Dupontel was all too aware the Belgian industrialist and chocolate magnate had been one of King Leopold II's most sadistic enforcers in the Congo.

As for Odile, who had crossed the floor with supernatural speed to take her place at the table before Dupontel had got anywhere near it, her coquettishly fluttering eyelashes and air of mild ennui belied a heart as dark as deep-sea squid's ink, for over the centuries she had seduced and corrupted half the crowned heads of Europe with such verve and efficiency that she had likely caused more harm to humankind than the other four put together.

Dupontel preferred not to think of how many existences had been poisoned, literally and figuratively, thanks to the caprices of the infernal cabal ranged around the table. The number was certainly in the hundreds of thousands, probably even millions. In any case, he doubted they kept count, since they rarely spared so much as a passing thought for their victims.

He had heard a rumour, apparently connected to the bungled operation of the day that had just concluded, that there were big changes afoot - possibly a development of some sort that would enable them to wreak even more havoc than they wreaked already. He suppressed a shudder at the thought and fervently hoped that, when the time came, he would find himself on the side of the predators, rather than the prey.

Dupontel held his breath as Miss Pim got to her feet, her tiny frame easily dominating the room. She was dressed, as usual, in deepest black satin, which contrasted with her scarlet lipsticked mouth and unnaturally ageless face framed by a dark helmet of impeccably behaved hair. Around her neck was a preposterously baroque necklace, a funereal wreath set with emeralds that gleamed in the sinister mood lighting.

'Drink, Henri?'

'With pleasure,' he rasped, his throat suddenly dry. Was this destined to be his last indulgence? He decided he might as well savour it. 'Armagnac, if you please, Madame.'

She walked over to the filigree cocktail cabinet, her kitten heels click-clacking on the marble, and poured out a small crystal glass of amber liquid from a bottle with a label indicating that Dupontel would shortly be sampling the finest and most expensive Armagnac he had ever tasted.

Odile leant towards him and said, 'Perhaps you would like a cigarette as well. You're allowed to smoke in here, you know.' She held out a gold case - like most vampires, she preferred gold to silver, to which many of them were horribly allergic - and Dupontel helped himself to one of the green cigarettes ranged within, willing his hand to hold steady as she touched the tip with the flame from a brass lighter stolen from the walking corpse of an esteemed American essayist. The cigarette tasted like flue-roasted bile, of course, but he forced himself to look as though he was enjoying it.

Miss Pim returned to her place at the head of the table and pulled out a chair many times less substantial than the thronelike monstrosity she had reserved for herself. She gestured for Dupontel to sit down in it, and placed the glass of Armagnac on the table in front of him, just out of his reach. He eyed it covetously, waiting for the moment when he could lean over and pick it up.

Close up, he could see the fine grains of white powder on Miss Pim's face. Her eyes were ice blue and extremely piercing. He squirmed as they seemed to peer into his very soul and sift through the detritus they found there.

'You're probably wondering why we summoned you.'

Dupontel had his answer ready. 'If it's about what happened earlier today, please be aware I have already reprimanded the Watchers responsible for the unforgivable delay. In some cases, they have been relieved of their duty.'

An eerie sound gurgled up from Miss Pim's throat. Dupontel realised to his horror that she was chuckling. 'My dear Henri, I am sure you have punished the parties responsible in an appropriate manner. I have complete confidence in your diligence. But now, I need you to prove your loyalty once more.'

Uh-oh, thought Dupontel. Here it comes.

'I am at your disposal, Madame. Whatever is necessary.'

Claude Bellinger piped up in a throaty wheeze that sounded as if the smoke from a thousand witch-burnings had cured his windpipe. 'And yet *it* was here, in Paris. And you let *it* slip through your fingers.'

'We need you to retrieve it for us,' said Melisande.

'Of course,' said Dupontel. 'I'll make the arrangements straightaway.'

'A child,' said Odile. 'A small girl. I think even an oaf like you should be able to flush her out and bring her to us.'

'But not just *any* child,' said Miss Pim. 'A child we had long thought lost, but who turns out to be alive. We underestimated the lengths to which the Arthurians were prepared to go, the sacrifices they were willing to make to cloud our awareness of her existence.'

'A disobedient child, by all accounts,' said Dupontel. 'There were powerful seals on the tunnel, and it was she herself who broke them.'

'Really?' said Pierre. He had been looking bored, but was now suddenly interested. 'Perhaps we can count on the wench's co-operation.'

'I doubt it,' said Odile. 'Not with those vile hags poisoning her mind against us for the past fifteen years. Who knows what lies they've been telling her.'

'Feeble ones, evidently,' said Melisande. 'She wouldn't have broken the seal if she'd known what it was there for.'

'And what, er, was it there for?' asked Dupontel. 'Perhaps you could give me some indication of why you need her so urgently... Just so I can take the necessary precautions.'

He immediately regretted the words that had just come out of his mouth, because Miss Pim was frowning daintily. But Dupontel had barely registered the creases in her forehead before they had vanished, leaving it as smooth and unsullied as virgin silk.

'Just get her,' she said. 'This is a task for the day shift, and as you know, Henri, we all need our beauty sleep.' She paused. 'For the time being, anyway. Until we can put her to the use for which she was created.'

Dupontel finally spotted a window of opportunity and reached out to grab the Armagnac. He raised the glass to his lips, but before he could taste the amber liquid, it was whisked out of his hand by Odile, who threw back her head and downed the contents in one gulp. He managed to summon a faint smile, but inside he was seething. He would get his own back on Odile Villeneuve if it was the last thing he did.

'Manners, Odile,' said Miss Pim.

'We don't want him drunk on the job,' said Odile, licking her lips. 'Mmm, that was nice.'

'Don't tell me this baboon is due for promotion,' said Claude.

Dupontel looked around the table and realised to his annoyance that Bellinger was referring to him. Calling him a baboon! The nerve.

'He is indeed,' said Miss Pim. 'But not before he has brought the child to us. Do you think you manage that, Henri? It shouldn't be beyond even your limited capabilities.'

Dupontel nodded uncertainly, and gazed longingly at the cocktail cabinet where the Armagnac was stored. Seeing that no one seemed about to offer him a replacement, he resignedly got to his feet and embarked on the endless trek back towards the double doors.

As he toiled over the marble floor, trying and failing miserably to affect an insouciant swagger, he felt their eyes drilling into his back. It was an uncomfortable feeling, but he supposed it was a small price to pay for the rewards. Siding with evil had its drawbacks, but he could put up with a bit of childish name-calling, he supposed.

Later, as he stood on the balcony of his beautifully furnished apartment and watched the sun rise, he sipped from a glass of inferior Armagnac and pondered his next move.

Chapter 15
The Glass Giraffe

This wasn't so bad, thought Paula. It was certainly better than that horrible little dungeon. You would have to be a giant to bump your head on *this* ceiling, which slanted to a high peak, criss-crossed by dark wooden beams. And she felt less of a prisoner here, thanks to two windows, which opened out over silvery rooftops bristling with small red chimney pots that were now reflecting the slanting rays of the setting sun. Being in an attic was always preferable to being stuck in a basement.

But though the windows were neither barred nor locked, they were so narrow she could barely squeeze her head through them, let alone her shoulders. Even if they'd been wider, the roof fell away at such a slippery angle Paula couldn't see any way of scrambling down or making it over to one of the neighbouring rooftops without falling and breaking her neck. As for trying to attract the attention of passers-by, this wasn't an option either, because her view of street level was blocked by the edge of the roof and a rather flimsy-looking gutter. All she knew was that this was the seventh or eighth floor. But even this was guesswork; coming up in the lift, she'd lost count.

She surveyed the room. Perhaps there was something here she could use as a weapon? There was a big, ugly armoire, but the door was locked and she couldn't find a key. The walls were lined with bookshelves, but the books were old and fragile, bound in crumbling leather, and looked as though they might disintegrate if you as much as touched them, let alone tried to commandeer one for self-defence purposes. There were glass ornaments shaped like animals, and a jar full of marbles painted to look like eyeballs, and a tall vase full of plastic lilies covered in dust. Perhaps she could pelt someone with the marbles, or poke at them with a plastic lily...

But this was desperate stuff, she knew. She felt weary and listless, as though her fate were already sealed and there was nothing she could do about it. The furniture was old and worn, but at least the sofa with its fake leopardskin throw was big and comfortable, so she sank into it to ponder her next move. On the low table in front of her were a carafe of water and some glasses. She still had a pounding headache from whatever they'd dosed her with at the cemetery, but after a few gulps of water the pounding subsided into a mildly inconvenient thrum, like a bad earworm.

Only after she had gulped down several glassfuls did she have second thoughts about the water. What if it was drugged? But too late now. Anyhow, it tasted like regular water, so maybe that was all it was, and she did feel better for having been able to quench her thirst.

*****

Down in the cellar, hearing the key turning in the lock, she had almost fainted with terror. As the door creaked open, Paula steeled herself for the worst, expecting to see a monstrous hunchback or drooling ogre. So she was agreeably surprised when her visitor turned out to be a pleasant-faced young man in wire-rimmed spectacles and a well-cut suit, like someone dressed for his first day working in a posh bank.

No, Paula corrected herself: his first day managing the posh bank his family *owned*. The suit was *that* well tailored. She relaxed slightly. Maybe she could talk him into letting her go. She tried to arrange her features into an appealing expression, and said, 'I think someone must have made a mistake.'

When he smiled back at her and replied, 'I think you're right,' her spirits soared. At last! Someone who was on her side! All was not lost.

Then his smile turned into a frown, and as he stepped past her to peer into the shadows, Paula saw two other people in the doorway behind him: an older man in a tuxedo and bow tie, and a thin, elegant woman wearing a mink jacket over a silvery shift dress which Paula immediately coveted, even though it was being worn by someone who was almost certainly in league with her kidnappers.

'Where are the others?' asked Tuxedo Man.

'What others?' Paula did her best to sound ingenuous. 'It's just me here.'

Tuxedo Man barged past her and let out a French curse as he hit his head on the low ceiling. He stopped, rubbing his head. 'Where did they go?'

'You're for it now, Gabe,' Mink Jacket Woman said to the younger man. 'You let them get away.'

'I did nothing of the kind,' said Gabe. 'No one has been in or out for hours.' He looked quizzically at Paula. 'Where's your friend? And the other guy who was here - what happened to him?'

'You can't go around kidnapping people and locking them in dungeons like this,' said Paula, as haughtily as she could. 'I demand to see the British Ambassador!'

Mink Jacket Woman snickered and said something very rapidly in French before switching to English for Paula's benefit. 'Oh, I'm sure you *will* see him, sooner or later. But he's one of ours, so it won't do you any good.'

Gabe turned to Paula apologetically. 'Take no notice of Simone. She's just jealous.'

Paula was incredulous. 'Jealous? Of what?'

'Of your youth, and beauty. You *are* beautiful, you know. Perfect. Did no one ever tell you that?'

Actually, people were always telling Paula how pretty she was, but she decided not to admit to that right now. She'd always waved off such compliments, or turned them into a joke, but secretly she'd been storing them up in a private place inside her, so she could take them out and think about them whenever her confidence needed boosting, which was more often than even her closest friends realised.

Gabe smiled at her again. His eyes, which crinkled at the edges, were quite charming. 'Calling it a dungeon is *so* melodramatic. This is just a common or garden *cave.* Most buildings in Paris have them. It's where residents store their surplus furniture, or their winter clothing during the summer months, or their bottles of wine.'

'You locked me in!' said Paula.

'And clearly that was a mistake.' Gabe pouted apologetically. 'I am *so* sorry. But don't worry, we'll make it up to you.'

Tuxedo Man was sniffing around the shadows like a bloodhound. 'I knew it!' he said. 'Morphies! I can smell those little creeps a mile off. They stink almost as bad as you, Gabriel.'

Simone snickered again. 'Cut it out, Alphonse. You know he's sensitive about his personal hygiene.'

Comprehension dawned on the younger man's face, as well as surprise. He turned back to Paula. 'Your friend was a shapeshifter?'

'No!' said Paula. 'I mean, I don't know. One minute they were here, and then all of a sudden they weren't. Don't ask me. I don't understand it either.'

'They abandoned you!' said Simone. 'Such lovely friends you have!'

Paula shook her head. 'I insisted they went on without me. They said they'd come back for me later.'

Simone and Alphonse burst out laughing.

'Oh they'll be back all right,' said Alphonse. 'One way or another.' He kicked the wall petulantly, and a small piece of stone fell to the ground. It reminded Paula of the last she'd seen of Sam, and the thought made her feel giddy again. Had he really...? No, that just wasn't possible.

'Well, I suppose we'd better get you out of here,' said Gabe.

He held out his hand. Paula hesitated before taking it, but she didn't have many other options, and she was eager to get out of the dungeon. His grip was firm as he led her out into the passageway outside, which was lit by a low watt bulb.

'Watch your step,' he said.

It was good advice. Paula had to concentrate on where she was putting her feet as she followed him along an uneven floor strewn with rubble and bits of broken wood, though Simone appeared to have no trouble at all navigating the obstacles in her impossibly high heels. Alphonse brought up the rear, muttering irritably to himself.

The corridor was lined with doors made from the same sort of wired-together planks as the one Paula had just come through. She tried to look through the narrow gaps as they passed, wondering if anyone else was being held prisoner. The darkness on the other side of the doors was impenetrable, but her ears picked up strange noises - faint whimpering, scraping and growling, as though there were animals cooped up in there. She tried not to listen, but the sounds were making her increasingly nervous.

At last they reached the end of the passageway, where Gabe ushered her into a small old-fashioned lift. He followed her into the cage and wrenched the concertina door shut with an ugly screech of metal. It looked heavy, Paula thought: much too heavy for her to yank open quickly and make a run for it. Not that she would have known where to run.

Left on the other side of the grille, Simone put her hands on her hips. 'You expect us to *walk* up?'

Gabe shrugged. 'Or you can wait here and I'll send the lift back down. In any case, there isn't room for four.'

He pressed one of the buttons, and the cage began to judder upwards with a grinding noise, leaving Simone and Alphonse looking disgruntled in the basement.

As the lift went up, slowly and laboriously, Paula peered through the grille at the floors they passed and saw sombre passageways fitted with brown linoleum and shabby Art Deco lamps. On one floor, she glimpsed a young woman lugging a cello case; on another, an old man trying to wrangle a small pack of poodles with their leashes all tangled up. She thought about calling out to them, but Gabe was breathing down her neck, and she had no idea whose side these people were on anyway.

But mostly the hallways were deserted. Finally the lift shuddered to a stop. Gabe pulled the grille open and escorted her along another gloomy passageway.

'I think you'll find it more comfortable in here.' He opened a door and hustled her inside. 'Do take a seat. I have urgent business to attend to, but I'll be back soon, I promise.' Then he turned and hurried out, closing the door behind him.

As soon as he'd left, Paula went over and tried the doorknob. Locked. Of course it was. He'd locked her in. What had she expected? She was still a prisoner.

But at least this was better than the dungeon.

What a day, she thought, still not convinced she wasn't dreaming. She wondered where Sam was - and indeed *what* he was. Was he still a... pebble? Or had they managed to turn him back into a person? He'd felt solid enough when they'd been kissing in the graveyard. Paula shook her head and laughed softly to herself. Wait until she told everyone at school about this! Though perhaps she would leave out the bit about the kissing. If Philip or Millie ever found out, there was bound to be a scene. It had been fun hanging out with Sam, but she had never meant to *get off* with him, not like that. That had been a misstep and now she wished she could take it back. Maybe this was her punishment.

Paula wondered where Millie was now, and thought about how she had been acting strangely all day, and about the ugly pearl she'd found, and that crazy story about the waiter trying to kidnap her. Maybe it hadn't been so crazy after all. Paula wished now she had paid more attention.

After she'd quenched her thirst from the carafe of water, she leant back and the weariness took over, so she rested her eyelids and, before she knew it, she'd nodded off.

*****

What a peculiar dream, Paula thought. She'd been snogging Sam in a cemetery and they'd been kidnapped and Sam had turned himself into a pebble and...

With a groan of dismay, she sat up. It hadn't been a dream. It had actually happened! And Sam had... disappeared? She still couldn't get to grips with it. It seemed so unreal, and yet here she was, trapped in a strange room in Paris, and everything now wreathed in shadow, and outside the windows the rooftops were gleaming in the sickly light of a bulbous moon half-covered by long, thin night clouds.

How long had she been asleep? Her bones were complaining. The sofa was comfortable, but not *that* comfortable. Not as comfortable as her own bed. She suddenly felt so homesick it almost hurt.

From somewhere a long way beneath her feet she could hear a woman shouting.

'Gabriel! Gabriel! Gabriel!'

She had the impression the woman had been shouting for some time. Perhaps it was the shouting that had woken her. Or maybe it had been the *other* noise, this time from somewhere much closer...

From inside the room! It sounded like... growling? Was there a dog in here with her? Paula sat up straight, her heart pounding.

The shadows shifted.

Paula's heart stopped pounding and stood still as she realised there was a figure lurking in the darkness next to the ugly armoire.

'Who's there?' She tried to sound braver than she felt, but couldn't keep the wobble out of her voice.

A young man stepped from the shadows into the half-light. 'Only me.'

It was Gabe. Paula could have wept with relief. He'd promised to come back for her and here he was! But the relief promptly evaporated as she saw his face wasn't as pleasant as she remembered. He was still smiling, but now the smile made her blood run cold. The wire-rimmed spectacles had gone, and his eyes were gleaming an unnatural colour, somewhere between orange and yellow. Paula had never seen eyes like that before, and they chilled her to the bone. And now they were fixed on her.

She pushed herself off the sofa and, without taking her eyes off him, backed towards the bookshelves. She groped around blindly, felt something cold and hard, and grabbed it, holding it out in front of her defensively. It wasn't a knife, but it tapered into a point, so it was better than nothing.

Gabe wasn't impressed. His lip curled. 'Really? A giraffe?'

Paula looked down at the object in her hand. It was indeed a giraffe. A giraffe made of glass. It didn't look very dangerous, but maybe she could break the head off and make it sharper. She raised the ornament in what she hoped was a threatening manner. 'You'd better watch out! I know kung fu! *Giraffe fu!*

Gabe smirked and took another step towards her, hands held up in front of him like claws. His fingernails needed trimming. He didn't look like a young bank manager any more; now he looked like a...

Paula brandished the giraffe again. 'I'll use this if I have to!' But she had difficulty getting the words out.

Gabe laughed. It was a dreadful sound, like bubbling tar. 'You *are* perfect, you know.'

Paula didn't dare take her eyes off him, but part of her brain registered the sound of the door opening behind her, followed by a woman's voice raised in anger.

'Gabriel! Stop that *right now!* Go to your room this instant!'

Gabe seemed to shrink back to his normal size. He looked embarrassed, and scurried out of the room, his tail between his legs.

A *literal* tail, Paula realised with a start. Poking out from beneath the young man's well-tailored jacket was a long, furry, whip-thin *tail.*

It was only shock that kept her from laughing. This was getting nuttier by the second. Kidnapping. People turning into pebbles. And now, a man with a tail!

She turned gratefully to the newcomer. Her saviour was a ferociously well-groomed woman only a few years older than she was, but unlike Simone, her face was kind, and Paula immediately warmed to her. She was immaculately clad in a form-fitting black dress which caught the light as she moved, sending out faint shimmers of gold. The diamonds around her neck were so big they couldn't possibly be genuine.

Whoever these people are, thought Paula, *they certainly know how to dress.*

'I am *so sorry* about Gabriel,' the woman said to Paula. 'He gets like this when the moon is full. A bit of a handful, sometimes. I did tell them to keep him away from you, but shapeshifters never listen.'

Shapeshifters again, thought Paula. But Gabriel had seemed very different from Claudine, whose transformation into a rat had been weird and unsettling, but not remotely threatening.

The woman in the black dress lit a cigarette and crossed the room to perch on the sofa, patting the place next to her to indicate that Paula should sit down too. Paula's legs felt so weak she didn't need much persuading. The woman watched sympathetically.

'This must seem like a bad dream to you.'

'You read my mind,' said Paula, trying not to splutter as cigarette smoke wafted into her face.

'I don't have to read it,' said the woman. 'I too had an experience like yours. A long time ago, but I vividly recall how frightening it was, how disorientating, and how I just wanted to wake up, so that everything would be back to normal.'

Her make-up was flawlessly applied, though Paula couldn't understand why she needed it in the first place; her skin was unmarked by pimples, or large pores, or even freckles. It was surprising to see skin that perfect on someone who smoked. Paula had a few freckles across the bridge of her nose, and had never minded them, but now she wished they weren't there. She wanted skin as perfect as this woman's.

She decided this woman was her new role model - though maybe not the part of her that smoked.

'Thank you,' she said. 'Miss, er Mrs...'

'Call me Ava. I am so sorry. Mistakes have been made.'

'You can say that again.'

'You're Paula?'

'I am.' Paula wondered how the woman knew her name, as she couldn't remember having introduced herself to anyone.

Ava picked up the edge of Paula's scarf, as if to examine the small knots in the woolly fringe. '*The girl in the red scarf*, they said. The red scarf. This scarf, for example. I'm assuming it isn't yours.'

'Well, no,' said Paula. 'My friend lent it to me, because I was cold. And then we had to...'

'This friend...?'

'Millie.'

As soon as the name left her lips Paula regretted having said it out loud. It was really none of Ava's business whose scarf it was. It wasn't as though she had stolen it.

A small sigh escaped from Ava's mouth, which was painted scarlet, just a shade or two darker than the red of the scarf. 'Millie,' she said, sitting back with a faraway look in her emerald-coloured eyes. '*Millie*... And what is Millie's family name?'

Paula didn't think Millie's family name was any of Ava's business either, but she couldn't help herself. 'Greenwood. Millie Greenwood. You can call her if you like; she'll back me up. I have her number somewhere, in my phone. No wait, I don't know where my bag is. They must have taken it. Do you know where it is?'

Ava ignored the question. 'Greenwood,' she was repeating, as though the name was some sort of mystical incantation. 'Green... wood...' Her lips parted in a smile. 'Ah yes, of course.'

Paula was taken aback by the odd expression that passed over the woman's face, like a dark cloud obscuring the sun. But it was gone as suddenly as it had appeared, and everything was bright and sunny again.

'You will write to Millie Greenwood,' said Ava. 'Tell her what has happened to you.'

'I'll tell her when I see her,' Paula said firmly. 'As soon as I get home.'

'You *will* write to her,' said Ava, more slowly. 'To please me.'

'Why should I want to please you?' asked Paula, though even as she said it she realised she really did want to please Ava, very much. She yearned to win her approval, and her friendship. She couldn't help herself. The woman was smiling at her in a way that was so very kind, and compassionate, and sympathetic, and her diamonds were gleaming. Yes, they probably were genuine diamonds after all, thought Paula as she felt herself bathed in the warmth of thousand summers' days, beneath a blue sky and the drifting fluff of dandelions. She could almost hear the soft trickle of a distant stream, and the yapping of a Cocker Spaniel, and the joyful shouts of children racing empty yoghurt cartons in the flowing current, competing with each other to see whose would pass under the stone bridge first, and win the race.

It was a memory from Paula's own childhood, and it was as though the woman had plucked it out of her head and served it back to her.

Paula snapped back into reality. There was no blue sky, and the only sunlight was radiating from Ava's smile. Outside it was night, and she was trapped in a room far above the bustle of the city and its inhabitants.

'So they made a mistake,' said Paula, and the truth didn't so much dawn on her as pop uninvited into her head. 'They were supposed to kidnap Millie, but they got me instead.'

'That is correct.'

'But why? Why Millie? What has she ever done to anyone? She's barely even been out of her village!'

'Ah yes,' said Ava. 'The village.'

There was irony in her tone, though Paula couldn't imagine why. Bramblewood was the dullest place she'd ever been in. There was nothing remotely ironic about it.

'So you'll let me go? I promise I won't tell anyone.'

Ava shook her head sorrowfully. 'Alas, I'm afraid it's too late now. We couldn't possibly let you go. You know too much.'

'I don't know *anything!*' said Paula, raising her voice. 'I don't know what happened to Sam, and that naked girl, and the other guy who was in the cellar with us. I don't know what's going on, and I think it's about time you told me!'

'This whole affair is a ghastly mistake.' Ava looked pensive. 'And now they want me to dispose of you. As if getting rid of you would make up for their incompetence. Out of sight, out of mind, I suppose.'

Paula leapt to her feet and started yelling. 'Dispose... You mean *kill* me? You think you can just *kill* me? You cannot be serious! You can't do that!'

'Oh, but we can,' said Ava. She let a few beats pass before adding, 'But I'm not going to.'

'Oh thank you *very* much,' said Paula, heavy on the sarcasm. She flopped back on to the sofa again. This nightmare wasn't over, then. In fact, she had the feeling it was only just beginning.

Ava patted her on the knee. 'I like your spirit, Paula. And I truly think... No, I *know* that you'll be more use to us alive than dead. Though when I say alive...'

'If you lay a finger on me, my parents will hunt you down.'

Ava laughed, a musical trill that sounded like a light soprano clearing her throat in preparation for the big aria. 'Diana and John? No, I don't think so. They're dormants. Yes, you see, I've done my homework. I know who you are, and I know who your parents are. And, more to the point, I know *what* they are, even if they're not fully aware of it themselves.'

'Stop talking in stupid riddles!' Paula felt anger rising in her chest again. 'They'll be searching for me right now.'

'Au contraire.' Ava shook her head sadly. 'They've probably forgotten all about you. The hags will have seen to that.'

Paula couldn't believe what she was hearing. 'No way! They'll have reported my disappearance. They're probably already here in Paris. They'll be talking to the police...'

Ava shook her head again. 'You poor darling. So innocent. You don't know what you're up against, do you. Your friend... Millie... has fallen in with some very bad people, some very *selfish* people, who will stop at nothing to keep her to themselves. Do you understand? You and your parents mean nothing to them. As far as they're concerned, your family is just collateral damage. Do you think it was an accident that Millie gave you her scarf? Of course not! She knew exactly what she was doing.'

It was Paula's turn to shake her head. 'You're lying!' But she felt tears pricking at her eyes. Of course Millie hadn't done it on purpose... Or had she? Paula hadn't even wanted the stupid scarf. It didn't go with her jacket. But hadn't Millie insisted?

Paula couldn't help herself. She burst into tears.

Ava slipped an arm around her shoulders. At first Paula wanted to shake it off, but it felt too comforting. And heaven knows she needed some comfort right now. She looked into the woman's eyes, which were close to her own. Ava's face was young, but her eyes were bottomless pits of ancient wisdom, Paula saw that now. They weren't emerald-coloured at all. They were almost black, like gleaming pools of midnight. And Paula felt herself being drawn down into them, deeper and deeper.

'As I said, Paula, I like you,' Ava said, so softly that Paula started to wonder if she had actually spoken out loud. It seemed as though Ava's voice was in her mind now. 'You're young, beautiful, and ambitious, and you remind me of... me. We would make a good team. I think you'll enjoy living here, with me. I can show you such sights. And you can help us, I know you can. There are things you know, even if you don't know you know them.'

'Like what?'

Paula wasn't sure what was happening, but she felt lightheaded, as though she were about to pass out. She tried to tear her gaze away from Ava's, only to realise the woman's eyes were no longer there. Ava had adjusted her position, and now her head was resting lightly on Paula's shoulder.

'I don't feel very well,' said Paula.

'Don't worry,' said Ava. 'This may hurt a little, but it will soon be over, I promise.'

'What will...?

Ava's black hair smelled like flowers. The scent was quite intoxicating. Paula took a deep breath, but before she'd let it all the way out she felt Ava shift position again.

She was kissing Paula's neck.

Paula could feel the touch of Ava's lips, tickling her skin like butterfly wings. She'd always wondered what it would be like to be kissed by a woman, but not like this. This was not at all what she'd had in mind. She tried to summon the energy to protest, but the sensation was too delightful, and she realised she never wanted it to stop. This was wrong, oh, this was so very wrong. She'd only just met this woman and...

The agreeable tickling was replaced by a lacerating pain, as though the scratchy label on a new blouse had come adrift and had sliced into her neck.

'Ow!' said Paula. 'What the hell do you think you're...?'

But then the dizziness swept over her, and she really did pass out.

Chapter 16
Type X

Millie panicked at the unfamiliar surroundings before remembering where she was. The panic wasn't so surprising; this was the very first time she had ever spent a night away from home, even if her own bedroom was no more than a few feet away, on the other side of the shared wall. As far back as she could remember, she had never slept anywhere but in her own bed; Paula had once invited her to a sleepover but, predictably, her parents had nixed the idea.

Her parents. It all came back to her in a rush. At the thought of Marcus and Aurelia, she felt a stab of regret followed by a shiver of excitement, which was almost immediately quashed as she remembered everything that had happened in the past twenty-four hours, and that Paula and Sam had gone missing.

Still, she comforted herself, surely they would have turned up by now. She'd been asleep for what felt like a very long time. All sorts of things could have happened.

And then she saw the hands on the clock on the bedside table, and panicked even more. Almost noon! She leapt out of bed and rushed downstairs, almost tripping over the trailing bottoms of the pyjama trousers.

Tanith was in her kitchen, drinking coffee. On the table in front of her was an untidy pile of books, papers and notebooks, pens and pencils, next to a big plate of custard creams.

'Have they found Paula and Sam?'

Tanith shook her head. 'Not yet. But don't worry - they *will* be found. We've got our best people on it. Good morning, Millie! Sit down and have some brunch.'

'But I'm late for school!' wailed Millie.

Tanith smiled, but there were mauve shadows beneath her eyes. It looked as though she hadn't slept much. 'Probably best if you skip school for a few days. Don't worry, I called Miss Cooper this morning, and she agrees. You and I have a lot to talk about, and in any case, it won't be safe for you there until the glyphs have been replaced or upgraded. They're in tatters right now, and they absolutely must be fixed before we can even think about letting you go back. Scrambled eggs? Tea or coffee?'

Millie sat down at the table and helped herself to biscuits. With her mouth full she asked, 'Is Mallory Hall... like the village, then? A school you built from scratch...? By magic? Because that *was* magic I saw, last night, wasn't it...'

Tanith shook her head. 'No, the school really was built over a hundred years ago. We simply... customised it, you might say. Installed a new security system. Made a few changes so it would be safe for you.'

'Safe from what? What about the teachers? And the pupils? Do they know what's going on?'

Tanith shook her head again. 'Let's just say most of your teachers and classmates are from a particular... lineage. They don't know what's going on any more than you do. But some of the parents may have a vague suspicion. Some of them have latent skills, abilities a bit like ours. Most have inherited the genes, but their ancestors stopped using those abilities centuries ago, so few today are aware of them.'

'What about Mrs. O'Keefe? And Sam's parents? Do they know what's going on? They must be awfully worried.'

Tanith bit her lip and looked uncomfortable. 'We'll talk about that later. But right now I think you need some food inside you.'

Millie was bursting with questions, but forced herself to calm down and eat her eggs on toast, while Tanith continued to peer through her reading glasses at documents and print-outs, occasionally pausing to circle lines of text in red ink. It gave Millie a chance to round up her scattered thoughts and put them in order, so as soon as she had polished off the eggs, she asked, 'Why me?'

Tanith put down her pen and leant back in her chair. 'Because you're special, Millie. You've always been special.'

'I just thought I was normal.' Millie gulped down a mouthful of tea. 'Well, maybe not *that* normal. I wasn't allowed to go anywhere on my own. I just thought my parents were...' She corrected herself. 'Well, they're not my parents, are they. What should I call them now?'

'You mustn't blame Marcus and Aurelia. They were given a task to perform, and they performed it to perfection... Right up until yesterday morning.'

'So where are they now? Will I see them again?'

Tanith gazed at her evenly. 'They went back to where they came from.'

Millie paused, and remembered what she'd seen on the floor of her house the night before. She took a deep breath. 'The red dust?'

Tanith nodded. 'Yes, they returned to the earth from which they were summoned. But you needn't worry about them; they didn't suffer. To all intents and purposes they were regular people, just like you and me, but the ability to feel physical pain, or even psychological distress, wasn't a part of their organism.'

No wonder they'd never hugged her, Millie thought, as she tried to remember what her parents had felt like when she'd touched them. Which hadn't been often. But she'd pecked them on the cheek now and again. Had that been red earth she'd been kissing? How come she had never suspected a thing?

Her parents hadn't been human; they'd been golems.

And now they were gone, as if they'd never even been here, and she'd never even had a chance to say goodbye, or thank you, or whatever it was you were supposed to say to people made of earth.

Millie frowned as she made some mental calculations. 'So when you say yesterday morning...'

Tanith nodded again. 'At seven forty-three. When you broke the seal in the tunnel.'

Millie remembered her dizzy spell on the train, and gasped. 'So it *was* my fault! That was a seal? Why didn't you tell me it was there? I would never have broken it if I'd known!'

Tanith sighed. 'Of course it wasn't your fault. You mustn't think that. Of course you wouldn't have broken it if you'd known. And we ought to have told you. I wanted to, really I did, but here in Bramblewood we do things by committee, and the consensus was that the less you knew, the less danger you would be in.'

'Well, that backfired,' said Millie.

'Yes it did. And I'm sorry. We messed up, but for heaven's sake don't tell anyone I said that. No one likes to be told they made the wrong decision... Especially not Pardew.'

'He's in charge?'

Tanith laughed. 'No! Thank goodness. We're a sort of collective, and the rest of us usually manage to keep him in check. But as you've probably noticed, he's very strong-willed.'

Millie sipped her tea thoughtfully. After a good deal of sipping and thinking, she finally asked, 'So who are my parents? My *real* parents? Can I meet them.'

Tanith seemed to be choosing her words carefully. 'Alas no, you're an orphan, Millie. Your real parents died many years ago. Nearly sixteen years ago, in fact, just before you were brought here.'

Millie felt keen despair and a sense of futility welling up inside her. What was the point of all this, then? In a small voice, she asked, 'Do you even know who they were?'

There was an agonising pause before Tanith said, 'Nicolas and Evangeline Vertbois.' It sounded more like a confession than an announcement.

Millie gasped. She knew those names. 'I saw their grave! In Père Lachaise!'

Tanith looked surprised. Millie had told her Paula and Sam had gone missing in the cemetery, but she'd skipped over most of the details, such as seeing them snogging, and the dancing figure in wispy grey. She didn't like thinking about that, even now. Maybe it was better *not* to think about it. It had probably been her imagination anyway. Maybe it really had been Sissy Urquhart all along.

'Well I don't suppose you finding that grave would have been a coincidence,' said Tanith. 'Something must have led you to it.'

Millie tried to think back to the moment she'd stumbled across the Vertbois tombstone. 'It was one of the birds, I think. There were a lot of crows there.'

Tanith shot her a worried glance. 'Don't trust the crows. They must have wanted you to find it.

'I *knew* there was something weird about it! I remember the name, because it was Greenwood in French. *Vertbois!*' She looked at Tanith in excitement. 'Does that mean I'm French?'

'You are indeed.' Tanith laughed. 'I suppose we'll have to give you extra French lessons now.'

Millie didn't mind the prospect of extra French lessons at all. *I'm French!* she thought to herself. *This is just getting better and better!* And then she remembered Paula and Sam, and the triumph leaked out of her, leaving her feeling guilty for having forgotten about them, even if had only been for a few moments. She had no right to feel happy while they were still missing.

'Why did that man try to kidnap me?'

'Well, now we're getting down to it. I was hoping there would be more time to explain all this to you, because it's a lot to take in all at once. But time is something we no longer have...' Tanith paused, and seemed to working out where to start. 'Have you ever had a blood test, Millie?'

Millie thought back. She'd had all the usual vaccinations at Mallory Hall, along with everyone else, but she'd never been sick, not *really* sick. Just the usual coughs and colds, and a bout of chickenpox, but she'd quickly recovered from that. There had never been any reason for her to take a blood test. She shook her head.

'I don't even know what blood group I am,' she admitted.

'Your blood group is very rare,' said Tanith. 'Very rare indeed.'

'O Rhesus-Negative?' Millie had learnt about blood groups in Biology and knew O Rhesus-Negative was the rarest. 'Does this mean I'm a Universal Donor?'

'Even rarer than that,' said Tanith. 'So rare there isn't even an official medical term for it. In fact, you may be unique, though we do know there's at least one other person alive with blood similar to yours. But only similar, not identical: positive instead of negative. The Syndicate calls it Type X.'

'The Syndicate?'

'The bad guys, Millie. The people who tried to kidnap you. Otherwise known as Maison Pim. They're not just a fashion empire. That's just a front.'

'I don't understand,' said Millie. 'Why would they be interested in my blood?'

'Because it contains certain... properties,' Tanith said quietly. 'And they want those properties for themselves. Your blood would enable them to do all sorts of things they can't do right now, though heaven knows they're powerful enough already. Your blood, if they ever got hold of it, would make them even more powerful. And then there would be no stopping them, and the world would suffer horribly because of it. Even more than it's suffering now, I mean.'

Millie tried to absorb this troubling new information, and failed. Only one day earlier, she'd been Millie Greenwood, and perfectly normal. And now she was... 'So what's my name? My *real* name? I'm Millie... Vertbois? Not Greenwood?'

'Your real name is Camille Vertbois.' Tanith tilted her head. 'But I'll carry on calling you Millie, if that's OK with you.'

Millie nodded numbly. She didn't feel like a Camille. She still felt like Millie.

'So these Maison Pim people... want my blood.'

As she said the words out loud they sounded unreal to her ears.

'Don't worry,' said Tanith. 'We'll keep you safe. That's what we're here for. That's what *Bramblewood* is here for.'

'But they want to kill me!'

Tanith shook her head sorrowfully. 'No, no, they don't want to kill you. All they want from you is your blood, and you have to be alive for them to take it. And they would keep you alive for a very long time, or at least until they've found some way of artificially manufacturing blood like yours.' Tanith's voice faltered. 'They would keep you alive for centuries, if need be.'

'I don't understand,' Millie said again. 'What is this Syndicate? Who are they?'

Tanith sighed, and her mouth set in a grim line.

'They're vampires, Millie.'

End of Volume 1

ABOUT THE AUTHOR

Anne Billson is a film critic, novelist and photographer whose work has been widely published. She is also well known as a style icon, wicked spinster, evil feminist, and international cat-sitter.

Her books include horror novels *Suckers*, *Stiff Lips*, *The Ex*; *The Coming Thing* and *The Half Man*; monographs on the films *The Thing* and *Let the Right One In*; *Breast Man: A Conversation with Russ Meyer*; *Billson Film Database*; and *Cats on Film*.

In 1993 she was named one of Granta magazine's 'Best Young British Novelists'. From 1993 to 2001 she was film critic of the *Sunday Telegraph*. In 2015 she was named by the British Film Institute as one of '25 Female Film Critics Worth Celebrating'.

She has lived in London, Tokyo, Cambridge, Paris and Croydon, and now lives in Brussels. She likes frites, beer and chocolate.

She has three blogs:
Multiglom (the Billson blog)
Cats on Film (films that have cats in them)
L'Empire des Lumières (a blog about Belgium)

SUCKERS
a novel by Anne Billson

'Billson honours the rules of the genre, then proceeds to have fun with them... Dark, sharp, chic and very funny' (Christopher Fowler - *Time Out)*

'A superb satirist' (Salman Rushdie)

'Merits a post position on everybody's reading list, even those who don't usually like vampire stories. It isn't splatter fiction; it's an honest piece of literature' (Elliott Swanson - *Booklist)*

'A black and bloody celebration of wit, womanhood and slapstick, beautifully sustained to a thoroughly satisfying climax' (Chris Gilmore - *Interzone)*

'A very camp and hugely entertaining vampire novel' (Christie Hickman - *Midweek)*

'Wicked and vulgar and unsettling... rollicking knockabout gore... nasty and brutishly funny' (Patt Morrison - *Los Angeles Times)*

'Enchanting and ominous at the same time; a rare and impressive piece of literary juggling' (Jonathan Carroll)

'A distinctive, original and refreshing debut' (Kim Newman - *Starburst)*

STIFF LIPS
a novel by Anne Billson

'A slick and remarkably controlled performance which more than equals her satisfying first novel *Suckers*. Ghost tales invariably leave me cold. I read this one in a single highly enjoyable sitting' (Paul Rutman - *Sunday Telegraph)*

'With *Stiff Lips,* Billson overturns the clichés of the horror genre, establishing, in their stead, her own original voice' (Lucy O'Brien - *The Independent)*

'Sexy, sardonic and distinctly spooky... a tale to make you shiver - if you don't die laughing first' *(Cosmopolitan)*

'*Stiff Lips* achieves an authentic and unsettling nastiness' *(Sunday Times)*

'A vastly entertaining story... As well as being a successful ghost story, *Stiff Lips* is an amusing satire... Funny and spooky - an excellent combination' (Sophia Watson - *The Spectator)*

'An absolutely terrific ghost story, taut and well-written with vivid characters and a spot-on blackly comic/satirical vein that does not detract from the very effective horror' (Lynda Rucker)

'Very creepy, thoroughly modern ghost story about frenemies, real-estate envy, going-for-the-gold bitchery and what makes the perfect boyfriend' (Maitland McDonagh)

THE EX
a novel by Anne Billson

'Great wit, great dialogue, great scares, genuinely disturbing yet never less than thoroughly entertaining, this book is a terrific read' (Stephen Volk)

'... like a cross between M R James and Raymond Chandler with our hero employed to protect a prospective bride from her fiancés 'ex' who just happens to be dead... Laughs and scares come thick and fast and the whole thing speeds along like a vintage Rolls Royce' (R.T. Brown)

'Witty, blackly comic, pacy and original. Seedy anti-hero John Croydon is the supernatural version of Len Deighton's Harry Palmer. Or as if Harold Lloyd had strayed into *The Omen.* Slapstick as well as chills...Totally recommended' (Lawrence Jackson)

'a fast paced, supernatural detective novel with a welcome vein of black humour running through it' (Oliver Clarke)

'Another page-turning spine-chiller from the author of *Suckers*... contains Billson's usual mix of dark humour, social satire and imaginative creepiness (Simon Litton)

'Another clever, creepy, wickedly funny book from Anne Billson, a great follow-up to *Suckers* and *Stiff Lips*... A thoroughly entertaining read, jolly good fun' (Esther Sherman)

THE COMING THING
a novel by Anne Billson

'Nancy is an unsuccessful London actress whose life goes decidedly pear-shaped when she gets pregnant - with the Antichrist. Anne Billson's *The Coming Thing* is a hell of a romp. It's like an inventive, witty and fast-moving cocktail of Ealing Comedy, the *Final Destination* films, *The Plank*, '80s satire, and more' (Braz)

'*Rosemary's Baby* directed by Howard Hawks with a touch of *The Producers*? To be honest that probably doesn't do this novel justice. It is one of the most original horror novels I've read in a very long time. It is also one of the funniest.' (R.T. Brown)

'*The Coming Thing*, about the impending birth of the Antichrist (in pre-millennial London!) is so funny and more than a bit freaky. It manages to navigate the line between horror and comedy effortlessly. Imagine if Clive Barker had made *Notting Hill*, or if you threw both *Rosemary's Baby* and *Bridget Jones' Baby* into a literary playpen! Very much recommended as a hilarious and spooky page-turner'

'Irresistibly engaging, witty, and gruesome. The perfect treat for the intelligent horror fan'

'An entertaining romp full of jokes, action, scares and social commentary... lashings of gore' (S. Litton)

Printed in Great Britain
by Amazon

19996336R00139